AN
ANTHOLOGY

Suffolk
Reflections

Original stories inspired by
the waterways of East Anglia

Foreword by Simon Peachey
of The National Trust Flatford

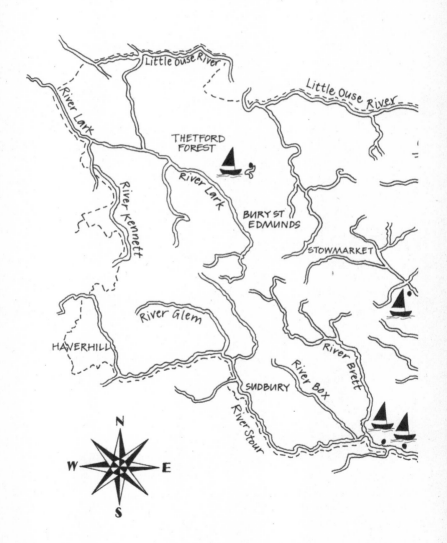

Suffolk Reflections Anthology
© 2023 Talking Shop Press. University of Suffolk.

All rights reserved. No part of this publication may be reproduced, distributed, or transmitted in any form or by any means, including photocopying, recording, or other electronic or mechanical methods, without the prior written permission of the publisher, except in the case of brief quotations embodied in critical reviews and certain other non-commercial uses permitted by copyright law. For permission requests, contact the University of Suffolk.

First edition 2023

Cover design and formatting www.jdsmith-design.com

Published by the University of Suffolk Talking Shop Press, Waterfront Building, 19 Neptune Quay, Ipswich IP4 1QJ

https://www.uos.ac.uk/courses/pg/ma-creative-and-critical-writing

Printed and bound in Great Britain by
Clays Ltd, Elcograf S.p.A

ISBN: 978-1-9989996-4-4

Welcome to our 2023 anthology *Suffolk Reflections*. This is the third in our series of anthologies of original stories from the Creative and Critical Writing postgraduate students at the University of Suffolk. These anthologies of new writing focus on the importance of place and illustrate the ways storytelling has such a vital role in our county's cultural traditions, past, present and future.

Our first and much loved anthology *Suffolk Folk*, took local myth and folktales as inspiration while the second anthology *Suffolk Arboretum*, looked at the ancient trees and woodlands of the county. This new collection *Suffolk Reflections*, brings an imaginative focus to the inland and coastal waters of the region.

The stories in *Suffolk Reflections* run deep through our county's meandering rivers, lakes, ponds, estuaries and seascapes. They offer the reader stories that bring to the surface the mysterious and fluid connections between bodies of water and the people who live alongside them.

In this anthology you will find stories to delight and reflect upon. In present day, a lonely woman and her child find a ghostly friend in the Blythburgh marshes. In 1940, two women must wait for love, watching a river flow between them. A child finds treasure in a dangerously rising current while the history of an ancient monastery competes with the primeval fears we have of monsters in the deep. In these pages you will find stories of desolate lighthouses, of the soothing power of the sea, of tide mills, and midnight summer swimming where the past washes up against the present in surprising ways.

The book includes a map along with the directions that feature in the introduction to each story so that it is possible to find every river bank, beach and waterway in the anthology. We recommend you set sail in your imagination with this beautiful book in hand, following the stories from the rivers to the sea.

As an addition to the anthology, we have also included the winning and shortlisted entries from the Student New Angle Prize 2023. This award is offered by the Ipswich Institute which runs the national New Angle Prize, and the Creative Suffolk Author Award sponsored by the University of Suffolk. These competitions celebrate writing that evokes the rich and varied cultural landscapes of Suffolk and the writers who live and work here.

We would like to thank Jane Dixon Smith for her help with book design and formatting, and everybody who worked on this book. Thank you to Dr Lindsey Scott Course Leader for the MA Creative and Critical Writing, for the title of the anthology, and to Amber Spalding for all her work in helping to edit and collate the collection. Finally, a thank you to all our writers for their imaginative storytelling and for being such an important part of a Creative Suffolk.

Dr Amanda Hodgkinson
Associate Professor English and Creative Writing
University of Suffolk 2023

Foreword by Simon Peachey, Site Manager of Flatford National Trust.

As the Site Manager at the National Trust at Flatford, I was honoured to be asked to write a foreword for this anthology of stories in *Suffolk Reflections*. It got me thinking about my own connections to Flatford, and Suffolk, and how the history of the landscapes I love has influenced creative people over the centuries.

Naturally I thought first about Flatford, and its most famous son, John Constable. I wondered, what influenced him to create some of the most famous landscape paintings of all time? Perhaps the answer lies in the landscape? In the early 1780s, he would walk to school each day across the fields from his home in East Bergholt to the Grammar School in Dedham. On his short journey, he would walk through a landscape of deep, tree-lined lanes, small en-closed fields and hidden hamlets. As the seasons changed, he would witness crops being sown, animals being fattened for food and the harvest being gathered in. This daily pilgrimage created a deep love and understanding of the countryside which he later translated into his paintings.

Although we are living some 200 years apart, I feel I know John Constable rather well. In my job working at

Flatford, I get to share the landscapes and waterways he loved most days of the year. Naturally, I had to seek out the story *Hope* in the anthology, set along the river at Flatford. In this beautiful story, the characters are escaping an apocalyptic future, finding refuge in the safety of the countryside at Flatford.

I recognised the sense of protectiveness and reassurance in the story itself, and am convinced that it touches on some of the reasons many people choose to visit Flatford today. In fact it was Constable's depiction of the landscapes he loved that put Flatford on the map as a tourist destination. His paintings came to represent a familiar version of the English landscape and a reference point of reassurance for many people through centuries of change and strife.

Another story which caught my interest in the anthology, was one which overlays the real events of the Sutton Hoo ship discovery with an engaging fictional creativity. *The King's Journey* is told through the voice of Basil Brown, the amateur Suffolk archaeologist who made the incredible discovery of the buried ship.

As with Flatford, I have a connection with Sutton Hoo. Not only did I used to work there for the National Trust, but my grandmother told me stories of her Girl Guide camp at Sutton in the summer of 1939, when she witnessed the shadow of a great ship in the Suffolk soil. At the time she didn't realise the significance of this great discovery and was unaware of the terror that was to grip Europe a few weeks later. However, it is this junction between peace and war, between security and vulnerability, which the writer considers in her story.

These are just two of the original stories I picked out from the anthology, but there are many more watery tales to enjoy in this collection, allowing us to travel to all corners of Suffolk through many centuries of history.

Although their subject matter is diverse, what unites them is that they are a celebration of local creativity. This is never more important than in this age of uncertainty, so I encourage you to pick up this book to start your own journey through the Suffolk landscape.

Contents

Lake Lothing, Lowestoft by Jayd Green

A few years ago, I stumbled across a number of articles, blog posts and photography centred around the abandoned fishing vessels and war boats that are dotted around Lake Lothing, a saltwater lake that forms part of the port of Lowestoft. The lake itself is part of the waterways that split the town in two, with the North and South parts connected by the Bascule Bridge and Oulton Broad Swing Bridge. A new bridge is being built, closer to the inner harbour while much of the port and industrial buildings that form the landscape of Lowestoft are closed. I wanted to write a story that incorporated this bridging of historical heritage and everyday attempts of intergenerational connection. Lake Lothing can be viewed from Lowestoft Marina, or by following Victoria Road up to the end of School Road.

Sunk by Jayd Green

In his youth, Dig had thought getting older would mean becoming more sure of himself and his place in the world. This was proving untrue. Oscar, his grandson, sat in the dinghy with his ill-fitting life jacket on. He complained and cried about it, until Dig told him that the coast guard would take the dinghy away unless he wore it. Of course, the coast guard was not watching them climb into the dinghy at Lake Lothing. Dig wasn't really sure where the coast guard would be, this early on in the year. Though the sun was out and blue skies all over, it was still too cold for many people to gather at the beach, and there were so few fishing vessels these days.

Oscar calmed, sat still and watchful. In the life jacket, he was bright as a berry. The sun reflected the orange plastic onto the boy's cheeks, like a buttercup held under the chin. Dig was rowing towards the wrecked boats but paused as two swans raced across the surface of the water to take flight. Oscar laughed at the slapping sound of the bird's rhythmic feet. Dig thought there was a certain enchantment of this water - a lake, with tendrils of ocean running through it. Sea-worn vessels rotted next to bust-up pleasure boats.

The water beneath them revealed what Oscar had come for: sunken pirate ships, where treasure might be found. Dig could have told the boy the real names and stories of the boats beneath them, but let the boy tell it instead, in his meandering, fairy-tale way.

They continued on, and the air became prickled and tangy. A newer, white boat floated by itself, lilting to one side. It was branded with caution tape, cordoned off by a bright blue rope.

While Oscar babbled on about a character he'd made up who had one eye but a lot of gold, Dig thought of his son.

Dig knew exactly where he was, had seen him just a few days ago, and yet. The gap between them had widened: Dig would get lost in the vastness of it while they attempted to string a long a conversation together, try to find the face of his son in the troubled man before him. Dig wondered whether his son felt like that white boat - cut-off, branded, dangerous.

Dig thought a lot about what his son was feeling, and had asked him last time he'd visited. Before entering his son's temporary room, he was cautioned by the psychiatrist that his son was still very much in crisis, but a little conversation with someone who loved him would go a long way.

Dig turned back to his grandson, who was here, and needed him too.

'How are you feeling, Oscar?'

'Happy!' The boy shouted.

His father had said, you've not asked me that in a long time.

Pakefield Beach by Daisy Woollerton

My story takes place on one of England's most easterly beaches: Pakefield beach. The waterway for coastal Suffolk is that of the North Sea, which I chose for this project as to me it symbolises a significant part of East Anglia's cultural heritage. That being the connection between Nordic and Celtic folklore, specifically the Selkie.

I chose to write about this beach, as I have lived in the area my whole life and Pakefield beach is a very important place to me. I would walk my dog here, I would go to small festivals on the cliffs and swim in the North Sea. During the summer of course... Even when I was at school, I would make up stories about what magical things were hiding in the sea and the sand dunes. As a family we would pick our way along the beach for sea-glass and lucky stones.

My beloved Pakefield beach resides tucked away between Lowestoft and Kessingland. When driving down the A12, before you reach Norfolk, head east towards Lowestoft and before you get to England's most easterly point you will find yourself on the pebbly Pakefield beach. On the cliff overlooking the sea, the church (and the churchyard sheep) stand. If you look out over the water, you may be lucky enough to see the sandbar and maybe some seals.

The Selkies of Pakefield Beach by Daisy Woollerton

I am going to tell you a story, my boy. A story of when I was a lad. About where we come from. You might laugh, but it is all true.

Do you see those cliffs. The crumbling green cliffs down the road? It starts there, just on the sand, underneath the church tower. I once had a night on the beach that changed my life.

It was late at night, June. I always used to visit the beach at night during the summer. The air was cooler and there wasn't a soul in sight. The moon, a waning gibbous, left a broken silver path along the water. I dreamed that swimming in the path of moonlight would be healing, the reflected light somehow imbuing the water with magic. It doesn't of course, the water is still salt water, healing and therapeutic in its own right, but not a mystical source that cures all ills.

That doesn't mean there isn't magic hidden underneath it.

That summer night I saw a seal. A small, greyish seal, popping its shiny head above the water. It was lit from the moon path. From the distance, I could see it blink its dark, pitch-black eyes and twitch its dripping whiskers. I blinked back on instinct, as if it were a cat. You know what cats are like, don't you lad?

I thought it couldn't have understood that I was showing

it that I meant no harm, but it stared at me still.

Have I told you about the mythical Selkie, my boy? The seals who shed their skin and transform into beautiful women. People don't know that they live in the water of the East Coast. Well, that seal I saw on the moonlight path was a selkie.

She had her coat stolen many years ago, by a fisherman. There aren't many fishermen here now, the old sheds, rusted boats and winches that litter the stony beach are evidence of that. I knew this creature wasn't a seal. Her eyes, as black and blank as they may appear, showed too much intelligence, too much pain. And I knew her.

That night, it was my eighteenth birthday. The argument I had with my own father was ringing in my ears. I had just stumbled my way to the beach from The Trowel, and after the night I'd had, I knew I needed to find her. So, when I walked past the church and down the winding path of the cliffs and saw her in the moonlight, I swam out to see her.

Now, I wouldn't recommend swimming, my boy. Don't you ever do it. But webbed hands and feet make even the most muddled minds sharp swimmers.

With a quick breaststroke I powered through the waves towards those dark, dark eyes. I never got her eyes. We have my father's blue eyes.

Seaweed tangled around my legs, and I stopped. My leg was paralysed by a cramp, and I was starting to swallow sea water.

I can hold my breath for a very long time, but in my panic, as I slipped below the dark waves, I gasped. The North Sea filled my mouth and my lungs, still cold in June. The light of the moon was shattered and swirling above me, slipping further away.

I don't remember much about the next few minutes, but I know that I was saved. A hand grabbing my shoulder, the rough grain of the sand, the water being forced out of me.

I found myself on the shore and opened my eyes, sore from the grit and salt. I saw a figure run back to the sea. A woman, slipping on a light grey fur coat, turned to me, the water up to her waist.

I told you that her eyes were sad, even now, as human as I'll ever see them. The only time I saw my mother, your grandmother, and she saved my life. I do mean it, my son, when I say we come from the ocean. We aren't just the sons of fisherman and sailors, but of the creatures of the sea. There is magic here.

The River Blyth by Daniel Snowling

Just a pebble-skim away from Southwold, to its east, and a slightly more ambitious stone-throw away from Halesworth, to its west, rests Blythburgh. A small village bisected by the A12 that sits among the marshland, mudflats, and estuary of the River Blyth. A large expanse of water that has long been closed to trade vessels and is now occupied by Avocets, Shelducks, and Lapwings, even Cormorants if you're lucky, or Herring Gulls if you're not so fortunate.

Hidden away in those Blythburgh reeds is a bird-watchers' hide. Such a place always caused me inexplicable curiosity growing up, and it was a sight I often saw on car journeys around my childhood town.

I grew up in the wetlands of East Anglia, so when I was asked to write a story that dealt with the waterways of Suffolk, I knew that I wanted to incorporate a piece of my childhood into it. The feeling of a quiet night by the water, encircled by reeds, a seclusion that is both safe and secretive.

When beginning this project, I thought a lot about stories from folklore and how they ripple through the families, societies, and cultures that remember them. I wanted the water to be a means of revealing. Revealing that which has come before and reflecting that which we already know. Through this piece I wanted to create a believable account of these ideas, as well as producing a folklore tale of my

own, one that, hopefully, will be carried on downstream.
I hope you enjoy reading.

The Lady on the Marsh by Daniel Snowling

I met Benjamin by chance that night and have thought a lot about what he said to me. Even now, after fifteen years of bringing the thoughts of that evening to mind, I still feel uneasy thinking of it. I remember there was a winter stillness that night, the moonlight shimmered on the water like pale flickering candlelight. The winding waterway was so calm it looked still, mirror-like, and the bright but thick mist made it hard to see where the water ended and the sky began.

Despite the main road and the houses that lined it being close-by, there was a remoteness to the marshes. The towering reeds could block all sights of Blythburgh and the river, and make you feel like you had found a secret escape from the world. I often wondered how many others had their own stories in this place, and how the trail and the water next to it connected them all together.

I had Matthew with me, as I often did back then. I remember he had trouble sleeping when he was that age, must have been no older than four, or maybe even three. The only thing that seemed to soothe him was being outside, something about the cold air and the peace and quiet, the effect of having two introverted parents I suppose. I still smile over how he used to think it was his God-given right to step and stamp and stomp in every muddy puddle along that path.

Looking back, it was probably an unsafe place for me to be, alone by the water with a young child to look after, but we had lived in the area for a while by then and I had started to feel comfortable with the water being so close to the house. So, the solitude didn't bother me, in fact it was always something that calmed me, much like it did Matthew.

Among the gentle, swirling reeds and the enveloping mist we walked down the narrow wood-decked path to the bird watching hut, or 'hide' as Benjamin told us they were *actually* called. The smell of salt and mud along the path always, until that night, felt like it was leading to some safe, long-forgotten harbour. Unlike any of our other nights spent walking there, a warm orange glow oozed like honey from the windows of the hide. Matthew raced ahead of me as if drawn in by the light. Without a word I followed him up the wooden walkway and watched him stop before the open doorway, standing in the orange glow.

'Oh,' he said, and looked back at me.

There was a man perched on a folding canvas stool that fishermen often have, despite there being a little wooden bench on the wall next to him. He was huddled in thick worn coats, had a plaid blanket draped over his legs, and a thermos next to him.

'I'm sorry for the intrusion,' I said. 'We just came to get some air and maybe see the birds.'

'It's no bother, really, would you like a look through these?' said the man, offering Matthew a pair of binoculars.

'What's your name, little man?'

I waited for Matthew to respond but he was still making his mind up about this stranger.

'This is Matthew, I'm Hazel.'

'Benjamin,' he said. 'I have some warm milk, if he would like some?'

13

Matthew was more than happy to accept the milk Benjamin had in his thermos. The steam swirled into the misty air as he poured Matthew a cup.

I sat on the bench opposite Benjamin who looked out periodically towards the waterway.

'Why are you out here. At this time?' said Benjamin.

I explained how Matthew was having sleep trouble and he said he understood. I also asked him why he was out here at this hour. It was too late to see any birds and I remember thinking, although I didn't say so, that he was tucked into the corner so far he was almost hiding from the birds.

'It's not the birds I'm looking for,' said Benjamin. 'On this night, every year, for the past forty years, a woman appears, standing there on the water's edge.'

I followed his pointed finger.

Matthew had started to feel very tired, and I brought him up onto my lap. He nestled into the lining of my puffer parka and at some point, soon after, fell asleep.

'See, she doesn't ever walk here,' said Benjamin. 'Instead she just appears, wading in the shallows until the sun rises and the sky lightens, then she disappears into the water.'

'Who is she, this woman?' I asked.

After some time he answered.

'The story is that she lost her son, many years ago. That he one day didn't come home, so she started looking for him.'

'What mother wouldn't?' I said instantly.

'She searched for days in the village, asking everyone if they had seen her boy, pleading for help. Weeks passed and she still couldn't find him. She had searched everywhere she could think of until she came to the water, and so she swam into the cold depths, diving down, again and again to find her son, until one day, driven to madness for her lost child, she never came back up.'

I looked at the still water as he told the story and thought about the long-sunken memories nestled beneath the rippling tides. The stories they keep in their currents and the way they trickle from one person to another.

Benjamin looked down to Matthew sleeping. He looked with distant eyes as his lips twitched a sorrowful smile. At this he wished us both a pleasant night and, taking a final look out the window towards the shoreline, left us. His footsteps on the wooden path outside faded into the night, but the story stayed with me.

I looked down at Matthew, stroked his hair and thought of how thankful I was to have him in my arms, and how I would feel if I ever lost him.

We were left in the darkness of the hide; Benjamin had taken his lamp with him and now it was just the dancing moonlight that shone around us.

A bright shimmer came from the water's edge, and I turned in my seat to see a woman standing there.

Her dress was such a pure white it seemed to glow as the moon did. The hanging fabric was floating around her as if she were dancing in a gentle swirling tide. She was looking out at the water and she paced the shoreline, her face never turning away.

Matthew was still fast asleep in my arms. I held him tighter than I ever had before, yet the thought never entered my mind that I should leave.

Then a sound came from her. A plea.

It was a sound without a source, as if it was itself an echo. One word. And with that one word I felt my heart sink to the depths of my chest. My face became flushed as if ready for tears.

The woman, still pacing on the water edge, still fixated on the waters, as if staring to find something, still pleading for some unseen thing, said only that one word.

'Benjamin.'

Minsmere by Molly-Kate Britton

Mikves are a body of 'living water,' meaning a natural collection of water, such as a spring, an ocean, or a river, though these details are often debated. These living waters are used for ritual purification, and water has long been considered in Judaism to be an instrument of God.

During and after WWII, the Jewish population in East Anglia grew exponentially, as Jewish people fled the Nazi regime. Suffolk was one of the many English counties that experienced a surge in the Jewish population at this time.

My river is the Minsmere, located in the nature reserve of the same name, near Eastbridge, Suffolk. As you follow the river east towards the sea, the ruins of Leiston Abbey will gradually come into view. The ruins themselves are a short walk from the river, and visible from the bank, but the heart of this story, and these characters, is in the water.

Minsmere 1945 by Molly-Kate Britton

'We call this a *mikve*,' Rachel explains, fingers ghosting the river. 'A natural flow of water, untouched by human hands. Even if you stuck your hands in, the water would still be untouched, because of how it moves.' Her hand dips into the river just slightly, and she feels the languid current brush her. 'We believe it's a gift from God. It heals, gives us life, shows His love.'

Rachel relishes the feeling of warm sun on her face and cool water on her hand. Julia's grey dress scratches against her arm. She's in her Sunday best, the long, thick, clothes she wears to church, and then to meet Rachel afterwards.

'Maybe that was why the old church flooded,' Julia muses. 'God loved it too much.'

With the sun beaming onto her blonde curls, Julia looks like the people in the windows of the new church, the ones with yellow stained glass around their heads. She prefers the old church, away from Julia's father and his insistence that he and Julia sit in the front row of the new church each week, while Rachel waits for Julia at the ruins.

The old church on the banks of the Minsmere is quiet, the building only a few brick walls brought to rubble by time. There is no place for Rachel to worship. No synagogue or shul, nothing since leaving London. But here Rachel feels God. Here with Julia, in the ruins, with one hand in the river. She imagines the water parting to reveal an old rope, covered in muck from the riverbed. A tangible tether to her people. Julia grabs her other hand, lacing their fingers, and Rachel feels that same rope binding them.

Here she is connected, to the earth, to her family, to her love, secured by twin ropes. 'My people, some of us, at least, believe when we die, we return to the water. That it protects us even in death.'

Julia sighs, rubbing Rachel's hand with her thumb. 'I'm going to a lake of fire,' she says, casually as if commenting on the weather.

She presses closer to the silent Rachel. They have had this conversation many times, and Julia has talked of fire and brimstone, of the teachings she hears every Sunday, before she comes to meet Rachel in the ruins, and then hears her father repeat over dinner. Julia decided long ago these moments by the river with Rachel are worth burning for.

Julia whispers Rachel's name. Rachel knows that tone, knows how Julia squeezes her palm, knows, without looking, that Julia has sat up ever so slightly, so she can watch Rachel's reaction to what must be bad news.

Rachel wants to stay here forever, clutching her twin ropes, far away from everything and everyone that would try to sever them. She pretends not to hear Julia talking of her father and a local boy turned war hero. She forces her eyes open and onto the elegant band that sits on Julia's finger. If Rachel tries, if she succeeds, between the sun on her face and cold on her fingers and Julia at her side, she could lose herself here. They could lose themselves together.

In the distance, Julia's father calls out, searching for his daughter. Julia pulls her hand from Rachel's. Sits up. Dusts herself off. Rachel's empty hand feels colder than the one the water, colder than the bank beneath. Julia places a kiss on her cheek and sets off running.

Rachel watches Julia leave, the flutter of her skirt and the streak of mud on her back, until she's little more than a blur under the arm of her father.

Rachel lingers a while, hoping the sun will return, swirling her fingers in the waters, until the chill seeps to her bones, and the light begins to fade.

Gathering herself, she walks home, fingers wrinkled and numb and shoved into her pocket, feeling the weight of her imaginary rope on her palm.

The next morning, over breakfast, Rachel skims the paper, and in black and white, she reads Julia's name in the announcement section, next to words like *engaged* and *church*. She drops her toast and excuses herself.

Julia is married in the new church the next Sunday. Rachel is standing outside when Julia and her husband leave, and Julia freezes on the steps. Her husband laughs, picks her up, and carries her to the car, and Rachel watches until they drive away.

Julia doesn't come to the river that Sunday, or the next.

Rachel sits alone on the bank and thinks about drowning. About sitting on the edge of the bank and tipping herself forwards until the water takes her, and that life-giving mikve takes away the life she no longer wants.

A man arrives at the boarding house the next day. He works for the grocer at the market. Jewish, like Rachel, and twenty-two, like Rachel, and he smiles bashfully at her, and Rachel supposes she could care for him.

The next Sunday, Julia is at the river, gold band glinting in the sun, and the two of them lay on the bank together as if Julia had merely changed her surname on a whim, and not as if she is someone's wife.

Two months later, Rachel has a band to match Julia's, and arrives at the river in her wedding clothes, a *mikve* before married life begins. The girls sit on the bank and

20

watch as their tears drip into the gentle current, and wish to be healed.

They meet every Sunday, as lines etch themselves into their faces, and their hair turns grey. When the time comes, when their husbands have died and their children are grown, they stand on the bank, the old chapel in view, and bind their wrists together with rope. They say their vows, exchange rings, and, rope trailing behind them, follow the river, wherever it leads.

Dunwich Beach by Kizzy Barrow

Dunwich beach has a particular place in my memory: it was a favourite spot for my family to park up before moving on to sites further up towards the North Norfolk coast. I've spent those whole blink-and-you'll-miss-them summers of childhood here, and as an adult I come back at least once a season, sleeping in the forest, on the heath or the beach. The bleak openness of the coast at Dunwich has always given me a fierce sense of abandon, like you might imagine the seabirds must feel, as they scream into the wind. To sleep with that wind pulling at the roof of the van, or buffeting a tent, to touch the phosphorescence in the wild dark sea- it gives me a sense of belonging, of ownership, but an ownership that goes both ways. It's a place that tells me what and who I am.

As common access to these wilder spaces dwindles, I think we must seek out these moments, in these places, and we must keep them and their magic alive- in more than memory. Claiming landscapes for our own is a vital and personal work. Don't let anyone tell you how, but I recommend straying from the path.

You can find Dunwich Beach by diverging from the Eel's Foot trail, if you like, and taking the path through Minsmere over the heath, past the coastguard cottages and teashop and along the cliffs. Or you can follow me down Monastery hill and smell the change in the air as you approach the sea. Stay the night if you can.

Pans, Bowls, and Even Our Hands by Kizzy Barrow

A dream? A moment that is at once forever and never. An impossible stretching of time in which you can turn like a fish, like a thought, darting to the threshold between sea and sky, never quite breaking the surface tension. Both liquid and not, held in a gentle breeze, suspended, rolled in the swell of some shallow ocean. An endless imperfect moment like this.

Follow me past the keep-out signs, dipping your hands into the moss that tops the fence as you jump it. There's that constant sound, the muttering of the sea– take a moment to realise it is not the muted roar of traffic. Pluck and crush a gorse flower between finger and thumb. A humming sound travels up your neck to reverberate in the hollows at the base of your skull, beating up from beneath your feet. When you step out of the sparse treeline it will shock you, like the sea spray leaping into your face, summiting the cliffs as the diving seabirds do.

Don't step there, to the left. The path erodes there, clods of spiny grass with sandy soil still held in their roots, tumbling into the sea. Even the lichen garlanded blackthorn and salt-worn gorse will topple and fall. Somehow, when nobody is watching, the coastline shrinks further from the sea with each passing year.

Follow me a little further along the path. It's the nineties, and I am a child. My home is the back of an old Mercedes van where I sleep in a cot below my sister's hammock, under a familial wool blanket that smells of diesel and tobacco. The wood panelled innards of the van are lit by tilly lamps. When we are on the road, they swing in great orbital circles and cast their light in ellipses and spirals over the things that are known.

We are the river flow, sing the Levellers. *We are the undertow*, sings my mother.

But this is not all that I know. Though the space, the contained things, the furniture that most people call home is small, my world is forests and oceans, standing stones and laybys and great fireside gatherings. This night, I sleep with the sound the engine sings to the sea.

I wake to a word. *Phosphorescence*. It's a word of science, but once it was my mother's word of magic, an invocation that brought the inky waves to life. My mother: brittle henna red hair, Alpha Blondy and Peggy Seeger at full volume, cursing and lullabies in a borrowed tongue.

She feverishly wakes me from the comfortable silence of dying embers and sleeping bodies, wrapping an old coat round the both of us and hustling along to the shoreline with pans and bowls. Wordlessly demonstrating, with hands clawed from cold, the lights that awake in the water.

The sun is descending, we're creeping into the liminal timeless time, but it is now, or soon, and you're here with me. We smell the sea before we see it. It's a vast, primitive, malevolent smell.

You make a silent stop where the road crests the cliffs, you know where we are now. To the right are ruins, a path flanked with creamy gorse. Here is the place with the ghostly sunken church bells, the drowned village. Somewhere around here are wild horses.

Let's take the coast path, which dips darkly inland, brushing the treeline of a forest before returning us to the sea's level. I cast out a trail of light behind me and you follow close behind. There's a trail of ragwort following the path here. If you push through them, you will dislodge dozens of the soft ribbed bodies of the cinnabar moth, fey horses that strip the plants bare.

At the land's edge, we draw together and swallow the raw iron taste in our mouths, the mineral sting of sea air. We are a small, laughing, light in the darkness with shadow-hollowed faces and the wind muttering like a drunk in our ear.

You start pulling at your shoelaces and we point our faces at one another, an answered question. I start pulling off my shorts, you peel off damp socks. We roughly lose the rest, flinging discarded clothes at one another in painful needling sprays of wet shingle.

I scoop up a double handful of the North Sea. A miniature galaxy is illuminated in my palms, splashing down my chest and leaving trailing embers on my raw skin. A moment alive in my hands. Now let me show you.

Feel the blood beat in your lips. You make an experimental pass in the water, a graceful arc, and countless tiny organisms respond to the movement. I close my fist in the water and lift it up above my head to watch them trickle out and pool with frantic brilliance at my feet. We duck beneath the searching rays that the lighthouse casts. To our right, the egg of Sizewell.

Now we are running, hysterically tripping over our heavy limbs, until we can wade no more and all at once we are plunging full length into the sea, grunting, and laughing and embracing and pulling each other over and under and over. The sunken village beneath our dangling feet. Gravity pulls, the tide pulls, the full moon's charm. From the luminescent sea to the horizon, faintly lit with shipping traffic, to the immeasurable fiery vastness above, and all of them joining together. There is no urgency, no movement beyond the arrangement of our bodies. It's the edge of the world, the corporeal limit. Any step in any direction might slip us through time to emerge, with bursting lungs, into a thousand other rivers or oceans.

From this ancestral sea I am drawn, with salt on my lips, by the call of my mother, the scream of a gull ringing on the wind. Open-mouthed and gasping, here between the sea and sky, I watch you roll into the waves, upright and strong. There is no other place we might be.

Huntingfield Waterways by Charlotte Yule

The village of Huntingfield, part of the Suffolk Coastal region in rural East Suffolk, is intertwined with networks of streams, and provides the setting for this story. The streams which lead past the lakes at Heveningham Hall, before merging into the River Blyth at Walpole, are an integral feature of village life, with many houses being surrounded by or backing onto the water. I wanted to capture the interaction between the residents and the water, specifically through the perspective of children who are often seen playing in the stream system.

In this story, a young girl called Essie wades the length of the waterways from the pool at the back of Blacksmiths Cottage on the edge of the village, round the back of Laundry Lane and under the hump bridge, before following the water upstream along the Carnser. Here she finds a treasure, a faded figurine lodged in the silt. As the rain arrives and the water levels rise, Essie must head for home, encountering the iconic Huntingfield Hare, a feature of the village sign and local folklore, on her travels. The village's main footpath, known locally as the Carsner, can be accessed at the hump bridge and provides a scenic woodland perspective of the waterways Essie explores.

Reflections by Charlotte Yule

Essie clutched the glass jar tightly as the current flowed over her hands. Her boots were submerged only up to halfway but somehow her socks were soaking wet. She repositioned her hands, shaking them gently so that the current rushed between her fingers and swilled the mud away. She pulled her find out of the water, examined it carefully and sighed. Now that the dirt had been washed away, she could see that it was just a piece of old brick, smoothed and rounded by the watery flows. She glanced at the empty bucket wedged between two rocks and decided that the brick was a start. It looked old after all.

She peered upstream and then down trying to decide which way to go. It was March and so the stream was at half flow, revealing all the treasures which lay undisturbed on its gravelly bed. Upstream she decided, and picking up her bucket, began to wade against the burbling water.

Essie thought she was probably up earlier than the other explorers, and that if she walked quickly, she could follow the stream round the edge of the garden, under the hump bridge and make her way to the bottom of the cottage gardens before the others had been allowed out to play.

The cottages, like every house in the village, all backed onto the stream. From this time of year onwards, with the stream running slower than in Winter, the explorers spent as much time in it as possible. It was drizzling slightly, and the droplets of water bounced over the stream casting ripples. Essie wished the sun would come out, the water shimmered like glass when it did, trapping the sun's rays within the sunken banks of the stream and warming the water so that flies and midges danced across the surface.

The bucket banged against her legs, swirled back and forth by the water's determination to get past her. Essie supposed she'd be in a hurry too, if she were the stream; eager to make her way far beyond the Carsner and out into the estuaries at Blythburgh, so she tried not to feel too cross that the bucket was hurting her shins, or that her feet were now so cold on account of the wet socks, that she couldn't feel her toes.

She ducked under the bridge, holding her breath in case a troll jumped out at her. She thought she'd seen one once, when she was out with Mum walking the dogs. Essie glanced around anxiously, looking for signs of movement under the water and hurried further on leaving the bridge and the possibility of monsters far behind her.

She was nearing the edge of the village and the stream had begun to meander, snaking around curved field boundaries. She had never been this far on her own before, and a hard knot weighed heavily in her stomach urging her to turn back. Just a little further she decided.

A noise in the undergrowth above startled her, a snap of twigs and flash of brown moving away at speed. She stumbled at the sudden noise, foot catching on something sticking out of the shingle awkwardly and clutched at the bank to steady herself. Her toe throbbed angrily in response, and she bent down to rub it, gasping at the shock of cold water over her hands. A flash of white in the deepest part of the stream caught her eye, glistening slightly.

Toe forgotten for a moment, she placed the bucket at the edge of the water and waded in, careful not to disturb the bed too much. About halfway out something pale glimmered, wedged partially under a large flat stone. She reached down, burying her fingers into the silt and gently eased the object free.

It was a figurine, a blue and white girl clutching a bucket of flowers. The face of the figurine was worn completely smooth, and the paint on her hands and skin was chipped to reveal yellowing white glaze underneath. The blue patterned dress was cracked in several places, with the corner of a fold chipped away, but Essie didn't mind. This was real treasure, a special discovery, made all by herself.

The rain had picked up, and Essie noticed that her boots were now two thirds submerged in the water. The stream was moving faster too, carrying small twigs it had grabbed from the banks as it started to rise, handfuls of forest giving way to the clutches of the water.

Essie looked through the trees ahead of her, squinting at the ribbon of tarmac which wound its way through the village, bordering the stream all the way. It shimmered with surface run off that poured off the fields, pooling at the sides of the lane until it had collected enough to rush over the banks of the Carsner, filling the stream up to the brim. Essie knew she needed to move quickly if the rain kept coming down like this.

Downstream the quiet was pierced suddenly by doors slamming shut as villagers began to emerge, drawn out of their houses by the falling rain and rising water. From the stream bed Essie had a perfect view of garden after garden as one by one canoes were carried up to sheds, pot plants moved onto higher ground and garden benches were weighed down with slabs and bricks. This was a well-prac-tised drill.

The water had risen almost three quarters up her boots now, and Essie grabbed her bucket, wading carefully to the stream's edge. In her hand she clutched the figurine tightly, feeling the ridges of the girl's dress hard against her palm. She scrambled up the bank and stood on the ridge, watching as the water picked up pace, frothing itself into foamy spray as it rushed against tree roots. Cautiously, a brown-nosed hare edged out of the brush, pausing to watch her warily for a moment.

'The Huntingfield Hare,' Essie gasped.

The animal startled, turned and loped away. Essie clutched her bucket tightly against her chest and broke into a run, feet pounding in pursuit of a flash of brown disappearing through the trees. Inside her tightly clutched fist, palm warm with exertion, Essie was certain she felt the small, faceless blue and white figurine, move.

The River Waveney by Ellen Freeman

The River Waveney forms a border between Norfolk and Suffolk. It runs near the village of Redgrave, passing by Bungay, Beccles and Oulton Broad before meeting the sea in Great Yarmouth. There are many ways to visit and enjoy the Waveney, including organised river tours, canoeing and wild swimming.

The Floods is a story set during the height of the Covid-19 pandemic. It is loosely based on my own experience moving from Norfolk to Suffolk - although I was an adult at the time, unlike my protagonist, Molly.

My choice to set this story on the Waveney was based upon the fact that it serves as a physical border between Norfolk and Suffolk. Molly is a curious and enthusiastic child, who has grown up in the city, and is struggling with the idea of moving into the countryside. Throughout the story Molly witnesses the beauty - and the destruction - of the river, as it floods. The gentleman in the story is also based on real life: the Waveney did flood during the Covid-19 lockdown and, while taking photos to explain to my boss why I couldn't leave the village, I saw a gentleman whose house had flooded quite badly. I wanted to use this experience within my story, but the situation was a little different in the eyes of Molly.

The Floods by Ellen Freeman

Molly had never given much thought to the fact that she had grown up in a city until she left it behind. She liked the loud music that played in the shops, and all the different things they sold. There were clothes shops, music shops, and sweet shops. There was even a shop that sold bears. It didn't sell anything else, not even other types of toys. It just sold bears. Ever since Covid had started making people ill, Molly hadn't been to the shops. The shops weren't even allowed to open at all. And there would be no bear shops near their new house.

Rain began to drizzle from the grey sky as they drove through the winding country lanes. All Molly could see was miles and miles of fields. There were sheep, and even cows in the fields closest to their new house, which she thought just about made up for the lack of bear shops. The rain hadn't stopped, and Molly watched in horror as the puddles on the roads became deeper and deeper.

Molly remembered her stepdad, Al, telling her that their new house was right next to a river called the Waveney. It was a river that flooded a lot, Al had told her.

Molly pushed herself up and peered further out of the window, trying to get a better view. The water was almost up to the top of the car's tires.

'The water will get in when we open the doors!' she groaned, looking at her favourite pink trainers. They were going to get wet and dirty.

'The new house is on a hill, Molly.' Her brother Max turned to face her from the front passenger seat. 'The water won't be deep on the hill.' Max gave her a reassuring smile before quickly returning to playing video games on his phone.

Molly sighed and turned back to the window.

'Wait, Mum, look!' she shrieked, pointing further down the road. Her mum slammed the brakes. 'That man's house has flooded! He's throwing buckets of water out the front door!'

The three of them sat quietly, looking at the house Molly was pointing at. Molly's mum frowned. 'I wish we could help him somehow.'

'He does look like he could use some help,' Molly agreed. 'He's quite old.' Molly started to open the car door but remembered the deep puddles.

Max turned around again, looking from his little sister to the old man, and back again. 'Molly, we can't go near strangers, remember? It was on the news, that... flu is making people ill. We have to stay away so it doesn't spread.'

Molly huffed. 'But his house has flooded!'

'I know, sweetheart,' her Mum sighed. 'But if one of us has Covid and doesn't know it yet, we could give it to him, and he'd get really poorly.'

'Because he's old?'

'Exactly.' Max nodded.

He was only two years older than Molly, but he often spoke as if he was a grown-up already. As Molly watched the old man emptying buckets of water onto the front porch, her mother started the car and they drove on through the flooded roads, towards their new house on the hill.

They reached the point where the river was supposed to

be, but you couldn't see the banks. The water reached right across the fields, and seemed to go on forever. The bridge had almost disappeared entirely, and they drove very slowly through the rushing water.

A procession of cars and moving vans pulled up to the bottom of the hill, where their new house stood at the very top, peering down at them. It was bigger than any house Molly had lived in before, and the hill looked very steep. Molly worried that once they got out, the cars might roll back down behind them. She jumped from the car and stared up at the big house in front of her.

Al waved her over. He was with Molly's mum, pulling things out of the back of his van. 'I've had an idea!'

'What are these for?' Molly asked, as Al handed her some blankets.

'We can bring some warm, dry blankets for the gentleman.' Al explained. 'I imagine most of his belongings will be too wet to be of any use.'

'I've called the local fire department.' Molly's mum helped her to pack the soft blankets into an empty packing box. 'They've added the gentleman to their list of people to visit today.'

Molly frowned. 'The fire department? But his house isn't on fire, it's flooding!'

'The fire department help with lots of emergencies, not just fires,' Max told her.

'Won't it be dangerous to drive through the water again?' Molly looked at her mum's car, the doors still dirty from their drive up to the house. There was a muddy brown line where the water had reached up over the tires.

'My van is bigger,' Al told her. 'The wheels are higher, so it will be easier to drive through the water.'

Molly squinted back towards the old man's house in the distance. 'I think I know how I'll make my first new friend.'

As they made their way down the road, Al's van slowly crept into the water. The swans were still gliding along, and Molly spotted a family of smaller birds too. 'Those are funny looking ducks.'

'They're not ducks, they're Moorhens,' Max told her. 'There are ducks on this side though,' he added, as Al stopped the van where the bridge ought to have been. Molly had never seen anything like it. The wind picked up, sending little ripples across the surface.

Molly had been worried that the countryside would be too quiet, compared to the busy rush of the city. But there were so many sounds. She rolled the window down to hear them better, and the rush of the water was almost as loud as the wind whipping past her. She could hear the ducks Max had told her about, and the swans with their little cygnets over the field. The sun peeked between the clouds, and she watched them swim peacefully through the glittering water.

River Alde by Charlie Brodie

This is a ghost story. I was largely inspired by the myths and superstitions that surround Iken, more specifically Saint Botolph's Church that sits overlooking the estuary of the River Alde. To get to St Botolph's Church, you can take the footpath along the river from Snape Maltings and keep walking east, passing Iken Hall, and crossing bridges, boardwalks, and when the tide is out, a beach. Once I heard about the 'devil phantoms' that plagued the river, I knew that I wanted to create a ghost story that plays with the boundaries of reality and believability like 'The Legend of Sleepy Hollow' by Washington Irving. My retelling recants the story of how Saint Botolph vanquished the 'devil phantoms' that hid in the marshes of Icanho, now known as Iken. At the time of his arrival, the site was a tidal island that was all but surrounded by the water. It is believed that the land was gifted to Saint Botolph – Botwulf – by King Onna to build a monastery, but when he arrived with his brethren, they were horrified to find that the land was haunted by eerie 'devils' that rose from the river Alde, and glowed in the night. There are few recollections of the events that transpired, but many believe that Saint Botolph charged into the possessed waters with cross in hand and exorcised the demons, bringing about peace to the land and baptising the river.

Devil Phantoms by Charlie Brodie

The river beckoned to me in a familiar, longing way, like the ringing of the bell that would call my brother and I to prayer. The resonant sound crept across the barren marshland and wrapped its gentle fingers tightly around me.

My brethren and I had returned from West Francia to the Kingdom of East Anglia, in hopes of building a monastery in this desolate wasteland. A gift from the late King Onna, a journey that only I could lead.

When I arrived here in Icanho, the brethren said the waters were haunted but I paid them no heed. And yet, I heard it too. The river whispered to me, asking me to wade into its waters and cleanse myself. I longed to be cradled in its arms, to be swept away and to sleep with the tide. Every day I came one step closer to the riverbank before jolting from its spell, stepping back from its grasp. Until the day I didn't.

It had started on the first night we arrived here. The brethren had felt it too, a presence creeping up their backs like ants on a hill. A layer of darkness cloaked the land, as if the sun had been stamped out of the sky. The winter trees, a series of monoliths extending their tainted arms to the sky as if in prayer.

It had dawned on us, as we arrived in Icanho, that suddenly there were no sounds. The sweet, simple chirping of birds had died on the wind as we arrived.

Life had fled Icanho.

We settled into the shadows, lighting a fire, and setting up camp for the night on the hill. River Alde lay dormant in the distance, the surface of the water motionless like a frozen pond. As we rested by the fire, the flames warming our calloused hands, much talk of death danced on the brethren's lips, passing back and forth in hushed whispers.

The Wuffinga King had fallen.

Grief sat with us, nestled in our hearts, as we spoke praises of the slain King.

I, however, was entranced by the flickering of the flames and the crackling of twigs. I did not hear the river at first, not until the brethren's voices dwindled out. The sound crawled up behind us and whispered into my ears.

An obnoxious odour had risen from the river. Bright green lights floated within the fog. *Devil phantoms*, the brethren had called these lights. I was enchanted by them. I sprang to my feet, wanting to be closer to the marshes.

It had once seemed darkly comical to me, a group of brethren trying to build a monastery in the presence of devil phantoms. I looked towards those swirling green lights and thought, perhaps the devil had arrived by boat and now hides in the marshes of the land. No sign of a wreckage.

That first night, the brethren kept the flames flickering long after we had fallen asleep, clutching their crosses.

The following nights passed in the same way. After a long gruelling day of building and prayers, the brethren and I sat around the fire, easing the knots that tied our bones together. A day of silence from the river bled into nights of whooshing water. It began to unsettle the brethren less and less, until the river was nothing to them. I, however, remained firmly in its grasp. It sung to me, a hymn that could not be placed, and on the eleventh night, the devil came.

I walked alongside the river following my nightly path when a scream pierced my ear; it ran through my skin and sunk deep into my chest. It was a short sound abruptly silenced, but the land echoed the scream. I looked to the looming fog that had coated the river. There in the shadows, wading in the waters, a figure stood. Its eyes bore into me. Two bright green orbs that rested in the air.

The singing of the water became tempestuous, flooding my body, filling my ears with a violent hum. I could not find the words to call for the brethren or to murmur a prayer, the river had stolen my voice.

The figure snaked invisible tendrils around me, pulling me, until the water was caressing my thighs. It enveloped into a hug that had no semblance of kindness. I stepped forward, as if possessed, and my legs were swiped out from under me. I was a pebble, dragged down by the current. Fragments of moonlight broke through the fog, briefly illuminating the murky water. I clawed at the tide, but it had no flesh to tear at, no arms to break out of. The devil was in the water, in the darkness that crept into my vision.

I reached for the cross nestled against my chest. It cut my palms. I began to chant a prayer, my chest burning as the water flooded my lungs, pulling me down into its silted bed. Darkness had swallowed my vision, but I could sense the presence in front of me, its hands resting on top of mine. They began to push at me, back in the direction I had entered the water, knocking the cross from my blood-streaked hands.

As I crawled back into the bosom of land, I emptied the water's poison from my body, retching until tears streaked down my face. The whispering water was silent. I had been baptised, faced with the demons of hell, and I had won. The water's spell on the land had broken, and the devils banished from Icanho.

Once I had finally caught my breath, I rose, turning to the river with a triumphant grin. I rushed to tell the brethren of my battle, shaking the water from my robes.

This land, now mine.

Orford Ness by Mike Laurence

Orford Ness is a long shingle spit of land which originates just south of Aldeburgh on the Suffolk coast, created by longshore drift over many centuries. It extends 10 miles southwards, diverting the river Alde far from its original outflow. It is now managed by the National Trust but was used for much secret military experimentation from the First World War onwards, notably the first attempts at bombing from aeroplanes, over-the horizon radar, and developments in atomic weapon detonators. It was home to a well-known lighthouse until coastal erosion required the building's demolition in 2020.

It is a place where the most disturbing aspects of humanity share space with wild nature, a landscape now being reclaimed by the non-human world. Many writers have found its lonely bleakness stimulates their imagination, perhaps the most well-known being WG Sebald's *The Rings of Saturn* and Robert MacFarlane's *The Wild Places*.

My own visits have always left me with an extraordinary hangover of mixed feelings quite unlike anywhere else. The opportunity to translate some of these emotions into prose was too good to miss.

It is open to the public from April to October, by boat from Orford. Outside of these times, it can be viewed from the coastal path across the river, in a way that perhaps increases its mystery, an inaccessible land of strangeness.

The Lighthouse by Mike Laurence

The distant masts stood a mile high above the mist. The falling tide carried the dinghy from the jetty, a pair of ducks moved effortlessly beside him. The cold air was damp and penetrating and Toby pulled up his coat zip the last half inch to his neck. It was a brief paddle across the inlet to the mud beach opposite. He stepped onto the rickety wooden landing stage, then dragged the rubber boat above the tide line, onto the shingle. No sound apart from a distant rhythmic wash of waves, and the occasional chitter of small birds searching amongst the stones.

Ahead was a short walk to the shore. No one around, the ministry warning signs saw to that. Toby looked up and down the thin spit of land. The Martello tower was just visible, a dark shape in the low mist to the north. He set his face east, to where he reckoned Sean would have walked, those months ago. No sign of him since, just gone.

Sean's dad had reckoned he'd moved away, but Toby wasn't so sure. He'd tried searching for his friend. The last address, a flat in a run-down terrace in Camden, was empty when he'd got there. A few boxes of Sean's stuff had been left on the doorstep for the charity collection. Toby had rummaged, found some scruffy T-shirts, and, at the bottom, a tatty notebook, Sean's handwriting for sure. Scraps of poetry, the odd sketch, some cosmic ramblings. One page stood out. A simple drawing of a tower– no, a lighthouse, a typical slim cone, striped, rotating beam indicated by faint lines.

Toby recalled a holiday they'd had, years ago, a sunny beach at Aldeburgh, and a long walk South, onto the Ness, past the squat Martello tower, then the path blocked by a high fence, MoD signs. He remembered seeing, in the distance, an odd collection of masts, buildings and beyond, a lonely red and white tower, flashing in counterpoint to the lighthouse further up the coast, stranded amongst town buildings.

It all lead to this point, here on the shingle, looking east. Mist hovered off the sea, a cold drift, obscuring the shore. He picked his way, uncertain. What clue could there possibly be on this desolate coast? His old friend had just disappeared, yet he'd been drawn to this place, this time.

He remembered the great times they'd had here, helped by magic mushrooms.

'With chemical mysticism,' Sean had said, as they'd watched creatures form in the clouds, 'who needs a Guru?'

They'd set each other off laughing until it hurt, with their backs to the base of the striped lighthouse, looking out to sea, in the warm salty breeze.

Sean had introduced him to it, of course, sex, drugs, festivals; all the great stuff in life, if he was honest.

Sean had wandered off before, when he'd been sectioned, but had turned up after a few days, dishevelled, off his meds, but quite cheerful, if a bit mad. This time, there'd been no news and here he was following a trail of memories.

Toby's gaze was drawn to a low concrete building, with an elevated lid, over to his right. The signs said *unexploded ordnance*. He reckoned the last time live bombs had been used was in the 1940s. Even so, he decided he'd tread lightly.

Inside, the room was surprisingly light, a weak sun cast low shadows on the wall above. Technical detritus was scattered about, coloured wires like fungal hyphae, seeking connection on the smooth surfaces around him. A smell of damp, rust, and a hint of rot. Metal cupboards and a rusted workbench were the most human objects left. He poked about for a while, until frustration, a heavy feeling in the pit of his abdomen, had him heading for the exit. Just before he passed through the doorless frame, he spotted an incongruence. A line of black writing, low down on his left, half obscured by a scrap of blue plastic sheet.

He squatted. The writing was very familiar.

It's gone, it's all gone

Toby stayed fixed to the spot, turning over fragments of memory, trying to imagine his friend's thoughts. Time passed, the daylight began to dim, and he felt the cold seep through his jeans. He slowly got to his feet, shaking his legs to release the numbness.

Sean had been here. A search revealed no more signs, just more rusty military remnants.

He walked out of the building, onto the shingle and wandered, unaware of direction, for hours it seemed, yet he felt no fatigue, no thirst and the shingle spit had no end.

He remembered a childhood dream he'd had, flying over a surface toward some distant destination, that feeling in his mouth, a pressure, still there when he awoke.

A breeze stiffened and he drew his jacket closer. The waves sounded nearby. A few little birds picked amongst the stones ahead, appearing out of the mist as he walked towards the sea. He thought of the lighthouse again, pulling at him, it had to be here somewhere.

Soft waves curled onto the shallow shore. A pile of rubble extended before him. Blocks, some with a red or white face, tumbled amongst ruptured concrete, twisted rebar.

The ruins of the tower. And yet he was sure he'd seen the

shape in the mist earlier, a winking eye of light.

The day dimmed as he walked slowly back to the little boat, and the sense of doom gradually lifted. Paddling back in the fading light, he felt the waters presence beneath him, a slick grey surface reflecting the darkening sky, the odd ripple suggesting activity below. A black cormorant sat on a rotting post on the far bank, wings spread, then lazily flapped off as he approached.

The feeling of loss grew again as he returned to the jetty. He knew Sean was gone for good, yet felt he was leaving his friend on a dead island behind him, left to wander amongst the stones and twisted metal.

Shingle Street by Claire Holland

As an area of outstanding natural beauty, and a designated Site of Special Scientific Interest, Shingle Street sits on the Suffolk coast, opposite the tip of Orford Ness, only eight miles northeast of Felixstowe and twelve miles east of Ipswich.

Shingle Street appeals to locals and visitors alike; with its remote location, the biodiversity of its flora and fauna, the abundance of wildlife such as nesting terns and its unusual coastal lagoons, all attract people to visit whether they want to walk, fish, swim, or bird watch.

The Suffolk coast and waterways have been a large part of my life; whether visiting the many Suffolk beaches as a child with my parents and grandparents, fishing with my dad and brother on the River Gipping, marrying my husband in Aldeburgh or walking along the banks of the River Orwell with my children. Being near the sea, listening to the waves and watching the ebb and flow of the tide has always induced a calm and tranquillity in me that I find soothing, giving me time to think, reflect and unburden myself. I wanted to write about a place unspoiled by the usual seaside trappings, somewhere remote where a visitor can find peace.

Travelling from Ipswich, Shingle Street can be found by following the A12, towards Woodbridge, then taking the B1083 to Sutton Hoo, before continuing along Heath Road to Hollesley and Shingle Street.

The Soothing Solitude of Shingle Street
by Claire Holland

Suffocated by the assault on my senses of my children bickering, my husband shouting at the referee whilst watching his football team getting thrashed on television, next door resuming their incessant drilling and the distant hum of traffic travelling on the A14, I feel overwhelmed, swamped, unable to think.

When I feel like this, I get in my car and head to the beach. The sound of the waves soothes my soul. Today, however, the beach nearest to where I live, Felixstowe, will be busy with families and dog walkers, wrapped up against the biting wind. What I need is somewhere devoid of seaside amusement arcades and rides, the air thick with the smell of chips, donuts, and candy floss. I crave solitude, seclusion, silence. There is only one place I know that can give me what I yearn for. Shingle Street.

Informing my family, I'm just popping to the shops, I get in my car and head towards Woodbridge, on the A12. It is then that I notice the petrol light blinking at me urgently from the dashboard. Luckily, there is a petrol station up ahead, and I pull in. Paying for my fuel, I impulsively purchase a packet of Marlborough Gold and a lighter. Although I have not smoked for years, not since my last cycle of depression, the urge in me is suddenly strong for a nicotine rush.

Refuelled, I continue my journey. Soon I am driving along the narrow country roads, before arriving at Shingle Street. I park just off the main road on uneven concrete, before a concrete ramp.

Getting out of my car, I walk slowly towards the ramp to the beach, a brown council sign stating: *Welcome to Shingle Street.* Already I feel more relaxed, away from the noisy chaos that is home. I stand still for a moment, listening. The only sounds I can hear are the waves and the wind, the silence, almost deafening me in its wake.

I sling my small bag across me and begin to trudge across the stones, my bag bouncing against my hip as I traverse the flint, shingle, and sandstone underfoot. The raw, natural beauty of the place, like the moderate wind sweeping across the shore, takes my breath away. Unspoiled coastline, the beach free of litter, the stillness of the place, exuding calm. I consider my surroundings: banks of shingle, like dunes, and unusual coastal lagoons.

I sit down next to one of the lagoons and look out to sea towards the spit. Orford Ness is just visible through the hazy mist that lingers in the air.

Further along the beach people are fishing. They remind me of my dad. I remember him regaling me with his tales of night fishing on this very beach, taking with him a flask of coffee, sandwiches made by my mum and him wearing layers of clothes including thermals, in a vain attempt to keep warm. I smile when I think of the occasion Mum found his ragworms wrapped in newspaper in the fridge, that he had placed on top of whatever we were due to have for dinner that evening. His night fishing days are over now, but I understand the attraction for him, sitting peacefully, with the sound of the waves gently lapping the shore, rod in hand, waiting for a bite, with only his small lamp for light when trying to place the bait on the hook.

I unwrap the cellophane on the cigarettes and after four attempts I succeed in lighting one in the increasing side wind, inhaling deeply. The taste of the cigarette is disgusting after many years of not smoking, but the nicotine rush is satisfying.

Sitting on the beach, alone, I have the space and solitude that I do not have at home, to mourn the baby I miscarried almost three years ago. The baby no one mentions, the baby I am relieved not to have and the baby I desperately want in equal measure.

Taking another deep drag of my cigarette, I try to reconcile the guilt I carry within me for those thoughts. My depression is severe, if the therapy is helping, I'm no longer sure, but at least for a few minutes a week I can offload how I am feeling to someone I have never met in person and in a few weeks, will have no contact with again.

A boy. The baby would have been a boy.

I think about the debilitating postnatal depression I suffered with my first two pregnancies, and I wonder if this time it might have been different, and I concede that I will never know.

Stubbing out my cigarette on the stones beside me, I pick up the butt, enclosing it in a tissue to put in a bin later. I pick up a small, oval, grey pebble, laced with delicate rings of white, smooth to the touch, my fingernails catching in the miniscule nicks and ponder how many times this small, insignificant pebble has been tossed and turned by the North Sea.

In the distance I spot an area out to sea where the sea is fighting against itself, the tide seemingly coming from multiple directions, hitting a shingle bank, and crashing over itself, exposing the shingle bank before it is covered by the sea once again.

Like the shingle bank I feel exposed and overwhelmed

in quick succession, unable to catch a moment's calm. Sometimes, I am like a lagoon, marooned amid a desert of shingle and shells, my life ebbing and flowing like the water within it. Sometimes I am full, at other times, I am low.

Feeling cold from sitting still, the wind chilling my bones, I stand up, but as I do so, I drop my lucky pebble. Instantly, I am irrational in my desire to find it once more. Carefully, I drop to my knees and begin the painstaking search for it.

The light is gently fading, and my search becomes more desperate, as though it holds some existential meaning to me and my life. I put the torch on my phone, and gently sweep the stones with its light.

At last, I spot the grey pebble laced with white rings and hold it close to me. I am comforted by its touch in my hand. I trudge across the flint, grit, and sandstone of Shingle Street, thinking to myself, maybe in life, you are sometimes marooned, but you must expose yourself to the elements, be trampled underfoot and passed over, to go along with the ebb and flow of life, before someone notices your beauty, your significance, holds you close, values you enough to search for you if they lose you, and are comforted by your touch.

The River Deben at Sutton Hoo
by Muriel Moore-Smith

Almost every Sunday when my children were small, we travelled from our home in East Ipswich towards Wood-bridge, down through Melton and up the hill towards Bawdsey. On the right, just past the roundabout, lies Sutton Hoo. The grounds there belong to The National Trust, but we used to treat them as our own private estate, enjoying as long a walk as little legs could manage followed by the inevitable trip to the café for a drink or ice cream. Some days there were re-enactments of the various events which make up the layers of Sutton Hoo's history: Basil Brown would dig in his tweed suit whilst incongruously King Raedwald prowled the site in his famous helmet. Other days, Basil Brown's bike was simply left leaning against the wall of his archaeologist's hut whilst inside a wireless played Chamberlain's chilling 1939 announcement informing us that this country was 'now at war with Germany.' My daughters began referring to Basil Brown as simply 'Basil,' as if he were an old family friend.

As they grew older, we stood near the burial mounds and looked down the hill towards the river. And when they were older still, we would walk with our dog alongside the path which runs parallel to the river. Looking across the water to Woodbridge, we would try to locate the various landmarks: The Tide Mill, the boat yard, which church tower belonged to which church. Meanwhile our dog would strain at the leash, desperate to chase the curlews or avocets or redshanks whose shrill calls were carried on the wind across the marshes and reed beds of the river.

After visiting Sutton Hoo on a school trip, my daughter related to us that Raedwald's ship was pulled up the hill on rollers made from tree trunks. We marvelled at the determination required to accomplish this task and marvelled equally, on a trip to The British Museum, at the intricate and majestic objects placed in the King's burial chamber by people from so long ago.

Now that my children are almost grown, I reflect on the way in which our own small family history is interwoven with that of this world-renowned archaeological site. My story *The King's Journey* tries to echo this: history and landscapes evolve, layer upon layer in time, yet remain parallel, almost within reach of lives lived in the present moment.

The King's Journey by Muriel Moore-Smith

Basil Brown leans his bicycle up against a tree and sits down on the spikey grass. It is not his custom to come to the riverbank to eat his lunch – usually he must tear off a gritty mouthful of bread whilst he digs – but today, after the Prime Minister Chamberlain's announcement on the wireless, he wanted to be alone.

He unwraps the wedge of bread and cheese from its greaseproof paper and takes a bite, purposefully chewing each mouthful. The river is peaceful, not silent: the halyards of the boats moored across the river slap relentlessly and somewhere unseen a curlew cries. When he was a lad, their call – the repeated piping up the scale - had made him feel lonely and bereft. It no longer does, having become merely one part of the vast symphony of sounds he associates with this stretch of the river. He traces the path of a pair of godwits making their way daintily across the skin of the wrinkled mud and there, along the sand bank, are the curlews who were calling, cunningly camouflaged against the reeds. He looks up at the Suffolk sky which hugs the horizon as far as the eye can see, admires how perfectly blue it is and how white the clouds which scud across its expanse. He looks at the glinting Tide Mill across the river at Woodbridge, the neat diminutive houses and church towers behind. Basil is not a well-travelled man – although he has read a great deal - but he perceives that these constituent parts make up a landscape which is unique. This place, which has barely changed for centuries, is his home.

Over a thousand years ago, when a ship carried the body of Raedwald the King up the Deben from Rendlesham to Sutton Hoo, the tide was high. The sailors, knowing the vastness of the task ahead of them, would have started out when stars still studded the sky, their eyes fixed on the horizon where the sun would surely rise. Forty men pulled on their oars as one. The boat slid silently through the water: the King's best oarsmen, used to traversing the water highways, sons of fathers who had arrived years before from across the great whale-road from far-away kingdoms. The land here is their home now, although they are boat builders, and the water is their true home. They have travelled and traded across continents, brought fine garnets and rubies and silver and gold from all over the world. These are now the objects which must accompany the King on his final journey, precious things to show his status in the land of the living, things he can barter with in the land of the dead.

On the riverbank, other men, strong men with shoulders used to pulling carts full of logs and stones, train their keen eyes on the river. They have been waiting for what seems like hours: the sun is hot on their heads, their limbs stiff from sitting. There is a shout: *Hey!*

A man, quickly followed by others, glimpses the golden carved dragon's head at the bow of the ship. Still only a promise in the distance, the King is coming at last. They are on their feet in an instant, shaking out legs, rubbing tight thighs, before striding into the water, heedless of the mud which sucks at their unshod feet.

On the river, a large raven flies just ahead of the ship. It looks down at the men on the shore with its beady black eyes and emits a piercing *caw-caw*, its wing tips spread like human fingers against the blue sky. *It is Woden*, murmur the men, pointing up at the great black bird, *come to keep his kinsmen Raedwald company on his final journey.* They shudder at the solemnity of this thing they are about to undertake.

It takes all of them, the forty oarsmen and the men on the shore to haul the majestic ship out of the mud up onto the bank. Women come with food and water to restore them, but they do not rest long. Shoulders pressed to the belly of the hull, hands on the still wet wood, they heave the ship up onto the tree trunks lying across the ground. The men pause, gasping for breath. *Watch out!* Someone shouts as the ship tips perilously, as if blown by a sudden wind. They manage to steady it just in time with the ropes attached to the bow and stern. The ship is made for water, not land: the keel which allows it to glide on the river cuts ruts into the wooden trunks; the lovingly planed planks of the hull are impossible to grip. Each weary step reminds them that this is the King's boat: large, heavy, perfectly constructed. They will be at the top of the hoo by sunset.

Wheeling his bike slowly up the hill towards the burial chamber, Basil marvels yet again at the feat of hauling the ship up it, the determination of the people to bury their king in this sacred place. Now of course, there are vehicles which would make this an easy task, amphibious tanks capable of crossing water and mud, able to ascend the hill in only a matter of minutes. He looks down river towards Felixstowe and the North Sea beyond. Landguard Fort is being readied, and the beach has been planted with anti-tank devices. Who knows if these efforts will be sufficient to stop an invading force? When Raedwald's forebears arrived here, they too were invaders from across the sea. Living, dying, being buried here: within a generation, this place became their home. The call of the curlew, the vast sky, the scudding clouds as familiar to them as it is to him now.

He turns to look at the river from the top of the hoo. Tonight, there will be no twinkling lights from across the water at Woodbridge: the blackout is already in force. As it was all those years ago, the moon and stars will be the only light by which to navigate. How carefully they lowered the ship into the earth, how thoughtfully they straightened the objects one last time in the burial chamber, ensuring that the King's helmet and double-edged sword were within reach when he awoke from his long slumber. Slowly, shovelful by shovelful, they would have piled the earth back on, before saying *farewell*, and leaving the ship to begin its journey through time.

Basil has one last task to perform: he must re-cover the ship, not with the earth that has cradled it for so long, but with bracken and branches. He reverently kneels and touches the darkened earth where the ghostly image of the ship lies. Raedwald's treasures have been hidden for safety in a sub-terranean chamber linking London's underground tunnels. He hopes the King can make his way without them, that they have been sufficient to allow him safe passage to his destination.

Branch by branch he covers the ship with the fragrant bracken until there is nothing left to see, only an indenta-tion in the earth. In the morning, he will ask the gardener to place some wooden posts around the site. He hates to think of the marauding young soldiers already billeted at Tranmer House falling into it, desecrating it, failing to appreciate that this is a sacred place where the past unfurls itself to the present.

Trimley Marshes by Emillie Simmons

Trimley Marshes is located at the end of Cordy's Lane in Trimley St. Mary, past Trimley St Mary train station on Station Road. There you will find a car park and gate, opposite a pond. This is where this story begins. To find the waterways located within the marshes, you would walk straight ahead of you, and you will reach the beginning of the waterway. Follow this and it will develop in various ways until you reach the River Orwell. This location is a serene and peaceful environment where you feel totally isolated, but also totally at peace.

This story follows a woman, named Sophia, on her walk through the Trimley Marshes and her reflections on her past and present life whilst also being submerged in nature. Sophia's character can take the place for many readers who feel burned by the pressures of society, and for those who find peace and clarity within nature. The Trimley Marshes for me are located right next to my childhood best friend's house. I have so many fond childhood memories in and surrounding these marshes and its accompanying nature reserve.

Sophia by Emillie Simmons

Sophia arrived at the gate entrance of Trimley Marshes, and she was immediately reminded of the time that she spent here as a child. The sun was setting, and, in the distance, the silhouettes of the docks covered the sky. The sun's amber rays reflected off the water that weaved its way through the marshes. The smell of freshly cut, wet grass and mud hit her face and took her back to the first time she has visited this place. Petrichor. A smell of innocence and freedom. As much freedom as child can have.

There have been times, though it was hard to believe, where the long grass had come alive, towering over her and fairies had flown around her head shouting '*Sophia! Sophia, can you hear us?*'

Sophia made her way along the footpath of the marshes and headed towards the wooded area. It felt like they were still here with her now. She was sure she could hear them faintly. '*Sophia? Is that you? It's been forever, please say it's you?*'

'It's me,' Sophia said to the setting sun and to the grass swaying in the wind. She whispered then, as if confessing something she had only realised herself. 'I am just a ghost of my child self.' But the fairies were not there, much to Sophia's despair.

As Sophia approached the wooded area, the marshes became darker. That is kind of like growing up and turning into a teenager - dark, scary, unknown. At least that's what it was like for Sophia anyway. No one warned her what being a teenager, or what growing up in general, was like. What it meant to be the eldest daughter.

This is the first time that Sophia has been back here since returning from university a few months ago. It's been six years since and so much has changed. The footpath barely exists now. The grass has overgrown. During her last visit, the nature was struggling to survive and so was she.

'Thank you, lockdown,' she said out loud to herself. The rejuvenated greenery energised her. It made her feel more at ease. The wind blowing through the trees and the water flowing nearby. Peace and tranquillity.

Sophia used to come here for an escape in her teens. It was a place in which she had some of her fondest childhood memories. A place where she felt that freedom. Now, she is a university graduate, living at home with her family and she needs that freedom that the marshes bring her. The freedom to be who she wants to be without any academic or financial, or social pressure. Without the pressure to do something world changing.

As a teen, Sophia used to come here to escape from the kids at school who ruled her life. What she wore, what she ate, what she said. But now her mother is the one controlling her. She doesn't let her go and do what she would like to without an explanation, and her father was at the other extreme and could not care less about what she does. And her sisters, well, that's a whole other situation. The marshes are Sophia's sanctuary. Her safe place, from everyone and everything.

In the dark the marshes look completely different, just like people and buildings do. The golden reflections of the sun are long gone, the silhouettes of the cranes at the docks are no longer visible and the water looks black, with the bright contrast of the moon's white reflection. Sophia knew she should feel cautious, being a woman in a secluded place in the dark. But she felt empowered, she felt like she could scream and shout as loud as she wanted and do whatever she wants, however she just sat with her thoughts.

Sophia thought, *I need to make my way back to my car. It's getting late and Mum will start to panic.* So, she did a one-hundred and eighty degrees turn and went back the way she came, following the clearing in the trees through the woodland area of the marshes. The rain began to fall gently and slowly, just grazing the bare skin on her face and the wind began to pick up. Leaves were beginning to fly and circle around her, giving Sophia an almost protective shield surrounding her.

As she broke through the clearing and was exposed to all of the elements, the rain began to come down harder. And harder, beating her skin rather than just grazing. Echoing as it hits the wet ground. Sophia picked up the pace, she did not bring a coat or an umbrella. Just herself, and her phone. It was darker than before, as the moon had now been covered by the rain clouds, so on went her torch. The peace and tranquillity that she felt before had now disappeared, and she was growing anxious of her mother and what she would say once Sophia returned home soaking wet. She began to run back to her car in the hopes she would be less wet than if she were to walk leisurely.

Sophia could see her car in the distance, and as she let out a sigh of relief, thunder erupted, and a light flashed throughout the sky. Her run developed into a sprint, becoming a race against nature to get back to her car and leave before the banks of the marshes burst in the heavy, stormy rain.

The Orwell Bridge by Sarah Waterson

The Orwell Bridge spans the River Orwell, which runs through the town of Ipswich in the county of Suffolk.

If coming from Ipswich by car, take the Wherstead Road, the A137, out of town, over Bourne Bridge, then turn left at the roundabout, onto the B1456. This road goes passed Fox's Marina and Boatyard, on your left. Keep going until under the Orwell Bridge, where there is a small layby, just beyond it on the left-hand side, where people can park their vehicles.

The bridge can also be reached from the A14. Take the exit at junction 56, then the A137 towards Ipswich. At the bottom of the hill, take the second exit on the roundabout onto the B1456. This road, also known as The Strand, goes under the bridge, beyond which is a layby on the left, where you can park.

Footpaths go up to and under the bridge. The walks take in the ever-changing tidal landscape and the many birds that can be found on, and around, the river. They also offer great views of the sweeping and elegant span of the bridge, and when standing underneath it, its size and strength can really be felt and appreciated.

Both the Orwell and its bridge are very special to me. When growing up, Mum and Dad would take me and my sister on outings along the river. As a teenager, I would take regular walks with my dad at weekends, and we observed the bridge as it developed and grew over the time it took to complete. Being an engineer, Dad loved the evolution of the bridge. He was so excited when we could walk over it.

This short piece is in memory of my dad and is dedicated to him, with much love.

In Spate by Sarah Waterson

Like water, father and daughter roll, like rills, over the smooth, soft surfaces of life.

Like water, their Sunday afternoon walks start at the headwater of their house on a hill, after Mum's hearty roast. Their motion is fluid as they trickle down through the suburban tributaries, circulating the island of the shopping centre, before spilling into the open concourse of the large, slopping park. Their walk becomes wider now, their strides expansive, their breath flowing into the seascape of the sky, before arriving at their destination, the river Orwell.

Laura was thirteen when she first stood with her father on the banks of the river, to watch the start of the build of the Orwell bridge. She is fifty-six now, but when she drives over the bridge or walks along the riverbank, she remembers herself, her father, and the bridge rising into the sky. Most weekends, back then, they would visit the slowly expanding leviathan. In fascination, they watched the progress of the free cantilever construction.

Dad was an excellent engineer, passionate about precision, enchanted by the emergence of the enigmatic form on the river that he loved. Whilst he looked forward to its completion, Laura found the growing structures both magical and monstrous.

Like the bridge, her own body was developing, growing out of the spring of her girlhood. She feared her own completion, too.

Laura had not sanctioned her physical transition. She could not accept something she had no power over. Without consultation, nature was forcing chaotic change, an assault of chemicals. The volatility of her moods, depending on where she was in her monthly cycle, the heady highs and crushing lows, the bloating, and her aching breasts, before her period, followed by menstrual cramps that reduced her to a writhing curl of pain.

Similarly, she thought, human beings were forcing a chaotic assault on the river and its ancient woodland, with concrete and steel.

Like a massive mechanical birth, the bridge pushed upwards and outwards, from deep within the broken earth into the future, its construction interrupting the flow of the river. The landing piers stood like regimented sentries holding the span of the bridge that started to cover the water coursing underneath it.

As Laura watched its striding, its stretching, she thought the bridge looked like a huge, long- necked, long-tailed dinosaur fossilised in concrete, forever held in mid-stride across the Orwell. She felt that perhaps the river itself may have known such creatures for real, in its movement through millennia.

Like the bridge, her body was long - her height inherited from her dad. She felt all unruly, bony, angular, a work making progress towards fulfilling expectations in the foreign land of the future. Though she longed for something other than this growing bridge, Laura had a deep sense that she too, was both ancient and brand new. This knowing enabled her to be moved by her dad's excitement when the bridge was finally complete.

On that day, father and daughter walked over the brand-new span in the excited crowds that had gathered. There was no vehicular drone, as cars were yet to cross it. There was just the gentle chatter of a sea of people ebbing and flowing above the river.

Like the DNA that courses through generations through the cycle of life and death, the bridge would carry people and their vehicles. Like blood thick with cargo, they flow through time, over tarmacked arteries from here to there, from past to present, to future.

Now, in her mid-fifties, Laura frequently crosses the bridge. And she remembers her youth and her late father, who remains a part of her poignant past. She is more than halfway through her own life, as he once was. These days, she can no longer remember the River Orwell without the bridge.

Throughout all this time, as Laura's life moved in ripples and waves, the river underneath similarly moved as it flowed towards Felixstowe and out into the grey North Sea.

When Laura is in her bed at night, she thinks of herself as a girl. She remembers her father, the engineer. She knows from deep within an ancient wisdom that the river is both the same, but different, just as the water that cycles around the planet, has always been the same, but different. It morphs and shifts through temperature, through motion and the movement of the moon.

Everything flows, like time, like familial DNA, like life and death, whilst the endless flow of human life is carried by the curves of a span over a river. It is the flow and fluctuation that cannot be captured in a moment, cannot be held like an ancient insect, in amber.

Laura turns in her bed, sleep pulling her down into depthless dreams, and feels that her own life cannot be stopped or destroyed.

She will continue to roll, like a rill, over the surface of life and then at an unknown point in the future, she will flow out into the wide, eternal sea once more.

Pin Mill by Jeni Neill

I discovered Pin Mill thirty-years ago, with my four-year-old daughter, dogs and 2CV. Settled within the Shotley Peninsula, you turn off the main road in Chelmondiston and drive downhill. Soon becoming our regular haunt, Sunday afternoons were whiled away amongst the splash of the shore and higher wooded path.

It's a timeless place, unchanged between those years and from the many before. The Butt & Oyster pub as reliable as the two boatyards and the row of eclectic Orwell River houseboats, some naturally shabby chic and a few contemporary. Rickety bridges and interestingly stilted platforms connect homes to the path. The houseboat in this story is a lone Dutch Barge though, by the Stour and Orwell walk which leads from the cottages, through the trees and over a couple of fields, before being spotted.

Pin Mill has a healing stillness, peace in its tidal respect of season and time, that has somehow escaped exploitation. Many an artist has taken inspiration from the scenery and spirit of the place, with the abandoned boat skeletons, exposed at low tide, like tilted whales' ribcages. *Swallows and Amazons* author, Arthur Ransome, famously set some of his novels here and his easily spotted *Nancy Blackett* is a regular visitor.

It seemed the perfect spot for my story's protagonist to settle; to root and be held by nature to reconnect with all that she was. I will see her here now, whenever I return, and nod my head to her with a broad smile. It's strange to think that she was here forming all those years ago, when I first walked down the hill and stood in wonder at the nestled hamlet that greeted me. And she has remained within me, for those years in between, waiting for her story to be released.

Silver Darlings by Jeni Neill

She was easy to miss, as she meandered the shoreline, her hair sandpiper brown. Delicate bittern-beak fingers finding silt covered treasures that hid in the endlessly wide horizon of loss – fossil, spearhead, dreamt Viking finds. The wind whipping her name away to tease and ride on waves of rough, savage sea.

Her mother's mind was absent, long returned to Scottish roots. For, years before, she'd moved to Lowestoft like the herring she'd come to slice and gut. Imagined escape through the foreign name she gave her girl, the woman became netted in a place not of her own, whilst her husband, disregarding, built trawlers for a trade all but dead. Unspoken despair hung like a weight in the growing girl's head and clung like the oil on smokehouse walls. She spent long days watching her silent father file, plane and saw and cupped sawdust dreams in her hands as they grew. So, with role-model lacking and sense of self thin, she was grateful to the boy who said she would do.

Wed, they made home by the sea; smelling of catch of the day with his waders drying over the fire. She embroidered their bedding with her initial G next to his A, trying to find intimacy for their sparce twiggy nest. It took them two-years of trying to accumulate loss. Knitted booties and hats left stored in the drawer – warming only the names of, first Fran, then Elena, Sasha, and finally, Roo. The shawl used only by the last, who made it to birth and stayed for five-days. Her soul roared with the rough savage sea.

Years passed slowly, grief pinning them down. She missed her husband's brief pause as he weighed his options before finally closing their door. Leaving her consumed in creating driftwood fish, with skills handed down, to form beautiful shapes from the sea's generous gift. She hummed a melodic tune of days now past as she traced her name through the wood carving curls.

Once her craft was perfected, she made four fish of sleek polished oak. Their shape tear-like as the spearhead she'd found as a child in the silt. These, she named her four lost ones, the darlings that had slipped from her hold. Their colours shimmered, reflecting the scales of her town's Silver Darlings and the depths that they knew - silver blending into hint of pink, yellow, green, kingfisher blue.

Packing her treasures to follow the change in the wind, travelling south along the coastline, to a place tucked well in. A hamlet, embracingly gentle in its pause of known time. She let the river's lung drag her, with its pull of the tide, the Orwell's channel tempts her to the strip of tidal muddied floor, where a sheltered community folded around the boat-mending shore.

From the Butt and Oyster, she walked back past the boatyards, cottages, down the path through the trees, with supplies and hopeful of making a living sketching for the visitors of this treasured spot. Over the small wooden bridge, she glimpsed a sight of her cabin-living, sunrising-orange, rocking retreat, sheltered from the endless hunger of space she'd always known.

She etched her name like a claim to the door, and lived in squelch, and wood for the fire. Her easel and bike dry under a tarp. The winters were battles but the springs came in song. Her carved driftwood fish dangling from her deck's pergola frame, covered in trailing nasturtium but still allowing light for her potted honeysuckle, roses, and herbs. Healing rhythm in the moon's gentle recall of tide and the salt marsh seabirds' annual return.

She knew when they came. Sea mist crept in, hanging low, weighted by all the sharp moments of loss she had known, dared dreams dashed before they had grown. A pot plant knocked on a windless night, the rocking roll of its lip the only noise to know or own, the others too deep for ear and yet heard within and all around, and in every cupboard and every tread.

Splayed in deckchair, she felt them close now, standing four in a row, staring intently at the four fish hung, as if longing to touch them, to feel where she'd worked. She knew, she felt in her bones, they needed her to look too, to see her four darlings, who had followed the strength of her calling heart while so lost at sea.

Long days passed with paint, books, and walks. Acrylic strokes swept over vessels tied to the Hard, to the path by the fields, to her bobbing Dutch barge, river view. Yet never breaking the surface, cutting the mirror, never forcing her dive. Some pressure was pulling, some magic at work. She felt warmth and connection as she deciphered herself, so unknown, and thanked her name for its spirit of the land and the sea; mingling now to hold her with love.

At the water's edge, where seaweed fronds and sucks the shore, all soft as playfulness tickles and caresses her dipped, sinking toes. Lowering her fingers, a child's hand slips into her own. Searching hard to define the translucent shapes within the ripples and swirls, the shifting aqua breaks creating a dance, creating an energy of sheer free delight. Whispering: *We're here, we're here.*

At the water's edge, cupping her hands full of dreams, they are there: wet as embryotic but free from the sac, slippery as new-borns gliding through the darkened depths. Gloriously basking, spread like stars, sliding back under to resurface once more. Dark ripples gifting light within the shimmer of her babes.

With each passing day this realisation grew, allowing all their names to fly free in release, replacing medical term and label of pain…no, not miscarriage but Fran. Elena, no longer an ectopic error, and the blighted ovum, never to form, was still her sweet Sasha. Dear little Roo, born too early, best kept inside, was re-birthed with his mother as she breathed him once more and filled her lungs with the sweet salt of their skin. She smiled to the river, knowing her trust in it was true. She had known her darlings would come back to her. She just had to wait.

They wake with her, rummage her paints, run on the mudflats, and raise salt marsh splash… She knows all their colours and tricks and dislikes. Each summer they draw to her and all cuddle in, she may read them poetry or sing old tunes of boatbuilding and fishermen, and how a mother's name can be heard in the voice of storms far-out at sea, of girls with hair the colour of sandpipers. All the long nights and the sleepy breath rising to the Autumn light now; orange glow from her fringed, shaded lamp and the fire crackle singing with the pings of the rain on the roof, which runs down over windows to encase this warm living womb.

There's a stillness inside that's calmed Genevieve's storm. Her name lies restored with her treasures, secure in her arms, having been snatched by the rough savage sea.

Neptune Quay by Luke Mayo

This is a story about Neptune Quay, the body of water located at the University of Suffolk. It can be found by walking out of Ipswich train station, turning right and walking for approximately ten minutes. Neptune Quay was once a working port and has evolved into a maritime hub of leisurely activity for boats. The area serves as the backdrop for the University of Suffolk, which is a key part of this story.

Waterfront Reminiscences by Luke Mayo

The morning was peaceful on Neptune Quay, but it didn't feel that way to Jeffrey.

He was making his way along the river towards the Waterfront Building. He would have been quicker, but for his easel and art supplies under one arm, and two folding chairs under the other.

Jeffrey panted and sweated, wondering why he was doing this. Then he felt a bright warmth on the side of his face. He looked at the harbour, the sun reflecting off the water and the boats filtering in and out, and he remembered why.

Upon reaching the Waterfront Building, Jeffrey prepared his equipment. He set the easel upon the stand, with the pencils and paper on the ground, and then he sat the chairs next to the easel.

This was it. Jeffrey was ready to be an artist.

It was quiet on this early morning in May. That was ok. More people would appear, and Jeffrey was sure they would love to have their portrait drawn. For now, he was content to look at that glorious marina, leading as it did to the sea.

Jeffrey sat with the Waterfront Building behind him and the University of Suffolk's Question Mark to his right. He was hardly going to be busy, so capturing that lovely view would be time well spent.

Retrieving a pencil, Jeffrey set about the job. His graphite strokes flitted across the paper, dancing in unison over the page in various shades. Before long, the Marina was sketched, depicting the sunlit port with a single boat setting determinedly away from the harbour.

Jeffrey grinned at that drawn boat, with a light optimism warming inside his heart. He imagined himself on the boat, heading away from his existence towards adventures. This thought made him happy.

'Hello?'

A man and woman stood beside his easel.

'Hello,' he responded.

The man cleared his throat. 'Are you an artist?'

'Yes, I am,' he told them. 'I come here every morning to do some drawing.'

The woman smiled, crouching to view Jeffrey's drawing.

Jeffrey smiled back, his eyebrows halfway up his forehead. He searched his memory for the last time his art was complimented, but nothing came to mind.

'Would you like me to draw you?' he asked. 'It would take ten minutes.'

The pair looked at each other. Bracing himself for rejection, Jeffrey glanced at his drawing of the departing boat, his yearning for a place on that boat stronger than ever.

'We'd love that,' the man said.

Twenty minutes later, Jeffrey was sat in the Hold Café with a coffee and some biscuits before him. He struggled to believe it: not only had he been asked for a drawing, but he had sold it for ten pounds. That money had been spent on the simple pleasures he was now enjoying.

Jeffrey looked around at the building he was sat in. He loved this place, along with the university and the Waterfront area. He saw creative works, heroic stories, and inspired ideas. Ever since he had first seen all this two years ago, Jeffrey knew this was what he wanted to be a part of.

He sighed, supping another mouthful of coffee. He gazed down at his easel beside him. The artistic world would never accept him. That had been decided long ago.

He closed his eyes, remembering what his mother told him when he was fifteen.

Jeffrey felt his lip wobble at the knowledge that he had not managed to do that.

Immediately after his mother's words, he had joined her working as a cleaner. His GCSEs slipped away beyond his reach, and he never entered a classroom again. He had hoped to join the University of Suffolk on their Fine Arts Degree. Fate had other ideas.

Months turned into years, and the cleaning work took up more time. Fortunately, with money in the bank, Jeffrey's mother got back on her feet, and they could both relax.

The problem was, Jeffrey had no qualifications, no experience, and no chance of getting the art degree he wanted.

That's what brought him to the Waterfront daily. He saw the place he longed for a part in, and he cherished it. He realised: if he could not use his art for a degree, he could use it for money.

Thus, the drawing business began. Jeffrey was now nineteen, and here he was. The degree was beyond him, but he was helping his mother with extra cash. He smiled, knowing this is what mattered.

Ten minutes passed, and Jeffrey was back on the Waterfront, art supplies ready. What few people were present drifted away. The afternoon progressed to evening. Nobody came, nobody asked for a drawing, nobody paid Jeffrey for his work. The sun set over the Marina, the boats still milling about. Looking sadly at the sky, the sun dropping over the horizon, Jeffrey started packing his materials away to head home.

'Excuse me?'

He recognised that voice. Walking towards Jeffrey was the couple from the morning. Their brisk pace got him wondering: did they want a refund?

The man held a booklet out to him. 'Take this,' he instructed. 'I'm glad you're here. You've got a real talent– why not look at our courses?'

Jeffrey held the booklet. The man's lanyard glistened in the evening sun. The couple left, and Jeffrey stared after them.

He looked out at the Marina. Jeffrey decided to set down his tools and use them. Pencil swirled across the paper, and before long, another picture of Neptune Quay was complete.

This time, the boat he drew was coming into harbour, and the passengers were smiling at the thought of coming home.

Jeffrey smiled too, sharing their delight.

Flatford Mill by Amber Spalding

Flatford Mill is a small hamlet nestled on the banks of the River Stour. It is a historically renowned rural idyll, capturing the likes of John Constable, whose painting *Flatford Mill* (1816) was his largest exhibition canvas to be painted, mainly outdoors. Scenes of rural Suffolk are immortalised through his art, depicting barges, boats, and their crew cruising along the Stour from Dedham Lock. You can reach Flatford by car - or foot, from neighbouring villages: East Bergholt, Dedham and Manningtree. When you arrive, stand on the bridge, and observe the river meandering downstream. Watch, as the water foams to the left – by the mill – and slows to the right, lapping up against the shore. Listen to the silence.

Water, woodlands, and wildlife were a huge part of my childhood. I grew up next to the water meadows in Sudbury, Suffolk, where too often, the River Stour would flood, leaving us trudging through waterlogged soil. I always believed there were stories here – washed up boats, slippery eels, mythical creatures, families, love – so many to tell. As a teenager, the Stour became our meeting point for bike rides, games of rounders, dates, parties. We *lived* there. And Flatford Mill is no different. My story images an apocalyptic future, where a mother and daughter search for safety downstream, meandering through Suffolk. The river leads them to this very spot, through troubled times, uncertain waters, loss, and love. All to survive.

Hope by Amber Spalding

It is spring and the tide is high. The Stour bulges from beneath, spilling over the vale; mysteries washed up on the riverbank.

It has been forty days since the fire.

Margot has been counting every one of them, watching the February sun bleed into March, then rise – slightly – into April, where the days are getting longer and the memories of Max slip into the shadows. It has been forty days since she last saw him. She remembers running for her life, sprinting through the forest with her child, not looking back, not even once. And somehow – among the chaos, she lost Max.

They left with nothing. They learned to build fires, to forage, to harvest rainwater. It was hard at first, learning to hunt for rabbits and deer. To Margot's surprise it was her daughter, Iris, who soon got the hang of it, taking the lead. She said she listened to the trees, that she could speak their language.

Margot and Iris move from place to place, people to people, from one side of the river to the other, crossing bridges, streams, wading through waterlogged soil. All to survive. Margot loses herself over and over, thinking about Max, but it is Iris who picks her up, carries her through the wilderness, teaching her a new meaning of love.

By her count, Margot is sure that today is April second. It'll take another forty days to reach the mouth of the river in Harwich, where she believes her daughter will be safe. She knows what she must do. Hold Iris tight. Head east until she can smell the sea salt.

She has no map. No compass. Nothing to guide her the way. The only thing she has– and trusts– is the river, easing its way through the vale, no rush. It knows it will survive.

Iris leads them through the edge of the forest; the ancient oaks– and there are many of them in Suffolk– give her directions to their new life. She listens to the elms and maple sing to each other and sometimes joins in, when her mother sleeps. She alone, hears their song.

It is almost dark by the time they arrive in the next village. The sun sets over by the water meadows, where Margot watches the cattle graze on the horizon, blissfully existing. Iris is over by the bridge, sitting on the edge. She can't see much into the distance, only the river lapping softly up against the bank and the odd starling in the sky, left behind, searching for home.

Morning comes, and with it brings a new landscape. Margot feels like she has walked into the scene of a painting, with the mill in the distance, foaming at the sight of an over-worked river. A family of ducklings glide along the surface, meandering downstream where it slows, too heavy to wave against the bank. There are oak trees too, half-in, half-out, trunks dipped black, growing from within the river. Their leaves turning green, thinking about spring.

Margot and her daughter walk over the bridge, down the lane, past the cottages, before reaching the mill itself. The water behind it is as still at midnight, so still, that when she waves her hand, it waves back to her. And it is in this perfect reflection does Margot see herself. *Not waving, but drowning*. She remembers the poem by Stevie Smith. It is a painful reminder of how close she is to losing this life.

Nobody heard him, the dead man.

She can't help but think of Max, the doubt, the loss, how bereft she feels without him. He would love this town, she thinks. The way the water tickles the shoreline, so peaceful, so welcoming.

Iris is getting hungry now, so they walk back to camp hoping to forage berries– though early, and catch fish. She will need some bait first.

But as they retrace their steps, Iris darts off to the left. Margot follows behind, but the girl is too fast, too determined.

'Iris!' She calls after her, running back down the lane, over the bridge, then left, across the riverwalk. She calls for her again - but being seven and unintentionally good at surviving – means Margot is left waiting.

Iris – seen from the corner of her mother's eye, dives straight into the spring tide, feeling the river bulge from beneath. It swallows her up for a second, then releases her like a sigh. She follows the meander left, where the beach thickens with silt, then disappears again.

Margot runs, fearful that her daughter too, is not waving but drowning. But there, coming towards her, is a narrow-boat. A girl. A man. Cruising along the river, back towards the bridge.

Iris

The girl feeds rope through her fingers, letting it drop into the water. The boat slows.

'Get off the boat!' Margot starts to panic; she can't lose the only thing she has left. She knows Suffolk isn't safe. She knows she's wasting time here.

It is only when she stands on the bridge, looking down at the water, does she know who the man on the boat is.

Max.

Margot jumps across the water onto the boat, flinging herself into his arms. 'How did you find us?'

'Iris,' he says.

The girl explains how she knows everything, the past and the future. How, over the last forty-one days, the river has led the family to this very spot. How she has laughed and danced with the trees while her mother slept. How the earth left a trail for her father. How they would always end up here by the river, reunited, at the beginning of their new lives.

But she doesn't say it like this, being seven years old.

'Hope,' Iris says instead, pointing to the hull of the boat where the crumbled paint reveals the word, so defined, so *right*, so obvious even, that everything now makes sense.

Hope is their future.

Needham Lake by Gabrielle Stones

I have always been drawn to Needham Lake. I (unintentionally) seem to have memories there at pinnacle times in my life. Starting from when I was younger, feeding (what felt like hundreds) of ducks with my grandma, to going there early hours of the morning with my college friends to watch the sunrise among the trees, to taking dog walks there now with my mum, and heading over for early morning Sunday car boot sales with my boyfriend. It's a place that has watched me grow up and has given me the same security I felt all those years ago. It's the first place I recommend and will continue to do so throughout my life.

Only ten minutes from Wood Farm Barns and Barges, exit the A14 at junction 51 and you will stumble across the lake as soon as you see the sign for Needham Market. It will also help to follow the sound of the geese!

The Days Gone by Gabrielle Stones

It was one of the warmest days of the year. The sun was beaming, glistening its way through our kitchen window. Marigold had her hair up in a loose ponytail, and the sun complimented her beautiful auburn hair. Her hair looked vibrant next to her pale white skin. Really, her whole existence was vibrant, like she was in partnership with the sun. She had the curtains wide open, and was enjoying her peppermint tea, staring out at the green on the trees.

'Do you fancy taking a walk?' Marigold chimed, facing towards me. I was slurping on my black coffee, with Otis placed in my arms, stroking his ear with my spare hand.

'A walk sounds lovely,' I replied with a smile.

Otis's ears stood on end as he heard us talk about a walk, his tail started to wag in excitement, and he pounced off my lap, barking on a loop. Marigold laughed, clutching at her mug.

'Somebody else likes the idea,' she smiled.

Everyone else must've had the same idea now that the sun was out. The sidewalks were packed with people, families, and other dogs. You could hear the silent sound of ducks from the lake close by, but masking that was the loud chatter of the town. Marigold was ahead, and she was the true view. She was wearing a beautiful cream and pale pink dress that sat just above her ankles. Her auburn hair poked out slightly from underneath her floppy straw hat, which had a pink and white striped ribbon around it. She turned to check we were still behind her, as if she could not hear Otis's hot panting. His tongue stuck out of his mouth and flapped in rhythm with his feet.

'What's the hold up? Come on, the lake is two minutes down this way.' Marigold pointed underneath a tunnel, where the other side was a picturesque view of ducks splashing around in water, families laughing together, and the sun flicking through the trees.

The view was lovely, so much so that I ignored Otis pulling to get through the tunnel, tugging my arm with force.

'Frank, watch him, will you?' Marigold yelled.

I pulled Otis's lead back to make him wait, but he charged forward instantly.

'Slow down love, he's pulling to catch up with you,' I replied, fighting the pull of the lead with every step.

Marigold walking, venturing under the tunnel, aiming her vision onto the lake in front us. Otis continued pulling, starting to choke himself with his lead.

'Marigold, wait, please!' I yelled. My voice echoed through the tunnel.

Marigold stopped at the end of the tunnel, her pale face adopting a red tint, warming to the sun. Otis caught up to her and jumped up in excitement, leaving trails of brown on her dress.

'Oh Frank, look! I have got mud all over my dress now!' Marigold scowled, rubbing at the dirt. In frustration, she turned round and stormed off towards the lake.

'What a joy.' I muttered to myself.

Otis didn't stop pulling until we got to the edge of the lake, his tail was at exceptional speed. There were other dogs around, but they didn't take an interest in one another.

Marigold was a few steps away, looking at the lake,

admiring the ripples that were created by the swimming flock of ducks. It amazed me she had such an elegance about her, even when she was frustrated. She was a beautiful addition to a lovely view.

Before I knew it, Otis jolted yet again on his lead, making me lose grip of the handle.

'Otis! Otis!' I chimed on repeat. We stood in shock as Otis leaped into the lake, creating a loud splash. His lead trailed behind him, almost mocking us for not being quick enough. His paws quickly rippled in and out of the water as he paddled towards a group of ducks. I could see the panic in Marigold's face. She began to wave her hands around and clutch at her summer hat.

'Frank, Frank, do something!' she yelped, edging closer to the lake.

I shook my head in disbelief, and at the same time I kicked my shoes off. Without a second thought, I plunged into the water. As gorgeous as the lake looked, it was different to be in it. I could feel weeds intertwined with my socks. I'd much rather watch the ducks paddle than imitate it myself, but there I was, paddling towards Otis, trying to keep my head above the water.

I could hear Marigold's screams, and I saw a crowd of families staring in my direction. No pressure.

I managed to grab hold of the lead and pull Otis back towards me. I paddled, with Otis in my arm, back towards Marigold. Otis kept his eyes fixated on the ducks he decided to dive in for.

I hurled myself out of the lake, shivering and soaking from head to toe. I placed Otis onto the ground, and he shook his white coat at great speed, spraying both myself and Marigold. She gasped and stepped back to try to avoid the water. But, without thought, I dragged her into a hug, uniting us with a watery embrace.

'Frank!' Marigold squealed.

I laughed, placing my arm around her shoulders. I kissed her wet cheek, and she smiled up at me. Otis jumped up out of jealousy, and Marigold picked him up, staining more of her beautiful dress.

Livermere Lake by Amber Atkinson

This lake offered inspiration for the story as it is a place where I took my own children to play during the first lockdown of the pandemic. I was encouraged to see the world through their eyes and learned how to find peace in the chaos by finding magic in the water.

Livermere Lake is located just south of RAF Honington and around four miles north-east of Bury St. Edmunds. If driving, it is best to park in Church Road near the War Memorial. Following the tree lined path with the Memorial behind you, will bring you to St. Peter's Church just beyond a white gate. After the gates, turn left to continue on the main path with the Lodge gates on your left. At the track, turn right and follow it into the Great Livermere Estate which takes you to the bridge where you can enjoy the views of the lake.

Ripple Effect by Amber Atkinson

The ripple effect is the greatest lesson a child can be taught. As an innocent child, skipping a stone sends magic wishes out onto its waters. As a mischievous teenager, it taunts those wishes out of you and threatens to expose them. As an adult, for every stone thrown across its glass plated form, a wish screams back at you as it dies. I like to think like the young ones do and believe in the magic of wishes cast on the waters here at Livermere Lake.

During what turned the world into a ghost town with no end in sight, the waters made wishes seem possible. A place children could escape into a world where this global panic did not exist.

The hottest summer brought with it, a restriction to stay inside apart from just one hour a day. Our one hour began with a fifteen-minute walk to the lake.

Within the tall green trees marking a boundary around a lake stretching so far across, the naked eye can't meet its end. This lake is home to ghost stories.

For Ashley, it's a place that keeps the fairies safe. The water never lies which means it also doesn't hide. As the white noise on the television and radio threatens to erase the world as we know it, escaping to the lake is like going down the rabbit hole. Today wasn't a day for the rabbit hole.

As we walked through the dried grass, an unfamiliar smell filled the summer air.

Ashley shouted, 'Quick! Race you!' And her small frame bolted as fast as she could to Mr Jingle's house.

Jess watched his sister and excitedly tried to run after her.

'Okay guys, let go find a spot by the water,' I said, unconvinced they would listen. The trees give homes to the songbirds and today their songs carry notes of everything we've lost.

'Mummy?'

'Yes baby?'

'Why can't we stay outside longer?' Ashley asked.

I put the brakes on the stroller and grunted whilst pulling out a blanket to eat on.

'The world is a little poorly right now Ash, so for now we just have to follow the rules and it will be over soon.'

'What if the unicorns fly all over the world and make people better and we can stay outside longer can't we?'

Wouldn't that be wonderful. Ashley often reminded me of the simpler times. Now all any of us had time to do was sit with ourselves. *Was it doing any good?* The world shut down and we were all living like we never had before. The quiet made me wonder, like many others, I am sure; *how did I get here?* I closed my eyes and tried to remember what being afraid of big things felt like when I was a little girl.

As a parent most questions are answered painfully. The last few months I'd begun to listen less to the incessant curiosities of my children and not answer most questions at all. Sitting by the lake and seeing my reflection in its surface, it taught me something.

I picked up a stone the size of a fifty-pence coin, and threw it frustratingly into the fragile mirror in front of me.

I dug my tired fingertips into the grass and warm soil, Jess sat between my legs, I closed my eyes for a moment. Ashley's snack bag began rustling, a less annoying than normal theme tune for the day.

I handed Ashley a smaller stone.

'Come here you two.'

I stood and walked my children, one in each hand, to the edge of the grass where we could be a little closer to the water. The unusually warm sun beat down on our faces.

'There's a secret about water that I think you should know. This lake grants wishes but only for people who are kind to it. Take this stone in your fingers and make a wish and then throw it as hard as you can into the water.'

Ashley was very bright for four and a half. She only needed to watch me a few times.

I held a little tighter to Jess and kissed his forehead as I sat to meet their height. There was a slight breeze that moved through our hair.

'I wish for the world to get better so we can go see Nanny Margot.'

They didn't know yet, that instead of going to see her as planned, my own mother and I were mourning Nanny Margot alone.

I watched as Ashley dug her bare wiggly toes into the grass, and cast her stone into the water.

Jess clapped excitedly 'Yay!'

Ashley screamed as she clapped.

'Every ripple you see on the water from the stone you threw, is how many fairies will hear your wish.'

'What will you wish for mummy?'

'I'll think about it a little longer, let's eat.'

The River Stour by Laura Cockhill

The beautiful and unspoilt village of Dedham lies within the borough of Colchester on the River Stour, and borders Essex and Suffolk. Starting from the nearby historic town of Manningtree, Dedham can be reached via a picturesque walk along the riverside, taking you through the heart of 'Constable County.' The river runs past Willy Lott's Cottage and Flatford Mill, which featured in John Constable's famous painting 'The Hay Wain.'

In the summer months, people flock to Dedham to hire traditional wooden rowing boats from the Boathouse in order to explore the Stour and enjoy views of the surrounding marshes and wildlife. The riverbank itself is a hive of activity, with many beautiful spots from which to sunbathe, picnic, and enjoy a spot of wild swimming.

Swimming in Silk by Laura Cockhill

It is unseasonably hot for May. The funeral finished hours ago, and I am alone again. My dress sticks needily to my back, and I can feel tiny rivulets of sweat running down the insides of my thighs, where I've been sitting hugging my knees for too long. From here the river looks reassuringly familiar, like overly stewed tea, almost amber under the late afternoon sun. I stand and lift the hem of my dress, padding barefoot down the incline of the dusty earthen bank. As I step into the cool restorative water, Robbie's face flashes in my mind, and my body tightens in response. I let my knees slowly buckle, slumping down into the water where I lay back, submerging my head so that only my eyes and nose remain above water. The sky is viciously, beautifully purple, the colour of fresh love bites. It sets the river alight and turns it a shimmering deep pink as the sun pierces hot and low through a haze of clouds. Suddenly, I think of Helen and the lump in my throat swells and throbs in response, so I feel as though I am choking. I push my head further under. The water fills my ears with a loud and consuming roar, until I cannot think anymore.

Robbie and I used to spend our summers sitting under the shade of the stooped old Willow. As teenagers, we liked to make fun of the tourists in their hired rowing boats, squawking as they crashed into one another or ploughed bow-first into the riverbank and got stuck. No one paid any attention to the 'Keep Right' signs. We liked to watch the men, tight lipped with furrowed brows, attempting to row in a straight line, or at least in the right direction, entirely humourless in the face of their laughing wives and screeching children. Occasionally a boat would float past with a man relaxing at the bow whilst his wife or girlfriend attempted to row them down river. We found the reversal of the classic gender roles hilarious, mostly because the women always turned out to be far superior rowers. After he left for Cambridge, I didn't watch the boats anymore.

Every summer without fail, Robbie came home to visit his mother. Most afternoons, he would take a stroll down to the riverbank and find me sitting under our willow, waiting for him. He always seemed surprised to see me, which somehow thrilled me even more. Sometimes he didn't appear and sometimes he had company, but occasionally he would come and sit with me, and it would almost feel like we were teenagers again. I often attempted to reminisce on our shared past, reminding him of our first kiss, or how he used to lick melted ice cream from my fingers as it dripped off the edges of the cone. I loved to see him blush and lived in quiet hope that one day he might find himself overcome with teenage nostalgia and try to kiss me again, but instead he always changed the subject. He would shift ever so slightly away from me, and begin to tell me something about his children, or *her*.

I hated it when he talked about Helen. In those moments, I would seek out an insect to watch; a dragonfly, with its electric rod body darting purposefully between reeds, or pond skaters, gliding weightlessly on top of the water's invisible membrane. I imagined Robbie and I as two pond skaters, living happily together on the river, dashing up and down like two starstruck lovers. In my imagination, Robbie and I were never just friends.

Today at the funeral, I finally saw Helen up close. (Previously I had only caught glimpses of her through a gap in my bedroom curtains.) Robbie had his hand on the small of her back. She was devastatingly beautiful. When he saw me at the back of the church, he gave a weak smile and nodded his head. I began to raise a hand to wave, but he had already turned back around. Slumping down at the end of the pew beside Mother's wheelchair, I felt suddenly small, as if I didn't really exist. I had desperately wanted to attend the wake, envisaging myself comforting Robbie and sharing the burden of his grief, like he had done for me all those years ago when my father died. I wanted us to be fourteen again, drinking tea in his mother's kitchen. Yesterday I had even taken the bus into Colchester and bought a black silk dress and high heeled sandals for the occasion, along with some Givenchy perfume and a new lipstick. What a waste of effort. At the conclusion of the service, Mother insisted we go straight home, convinced that her catheter wasn't correctly in situ, grumbling repeatedly about her *underskirt* and *leaking*. As I wheeled her down the street towards our red front door with its depressingly familiar old brass knocker, the tumbling down waterfall of ivy clinging to the brickwork, I felt as though I were marching myself back to prison.

I float on my back until the absence of sunlight turns the water chilly, slowly drifting back to the river's edge and hauling myself out. I grab my abandoned sandals from the grassy verge and begin to walk home just as the sun is collapsing beneath the fields, the hem of my black silk dress dripping a steady trail of river water onto the ground behind me. As I approach the main street, I see a 'For Sale' sign has been hammered into the front lawn of Elsbeth's garden, and that Robbie's car is no longer on the drive. The gates have been padlocked. Soon, a new family will live there. Someone else will sleep in the bedroom that was once Robbie's, and I will no longer see his silver Estate rolling onto the drive in the first week of the summer holidays, the only week I have marked on my calendar each year since he left for university thirty-two years ago.

The Student New Angle Prize
Writing Awards 2023

The Student New Angle Prize Winner 2023 Anya Page

I was inspired to write 'An Abandoned Airfield' by my research into the building of airbases in Suffolk during the Second World War, and the tensions and excitement of the war time presence of thousands of American service personnel in East Anglia. My story focuses on the constancy of nature, as well as the changing uses of the landscape. It imagines the lives of the people who dwelt, worked, loved, and died on a parcel of land in a corner of Suffolk. I hope that readers of 'An Abandoned Airfield' will share my sense of how the struggles and experiences of those who have lived before us leave an intangible trace, and my feeling that, in East Anglia, the past is always very close by, almost touchable.

An Abandoned Airfield by Anya Page

When the wind is blowing from the past, this seeming empty space comes back to life. A horseman whistles as he guides his horse, slowly churning perfect furrows into the soil. Screaming black headed gulls alight behind, picking at the fresh earth. Crops rise then sway golden in the sun, are reaped, threshed, gathered into stooks. Every man, woman, and child labours with aching back from first light until sundown. The weather holds. The barns are filled. The farmer's bank account swells and the bellies of the village children are relieved from the knots of hunger for a time. The church is full, thankful in song.

Look again, and row after row of khaki canvas tents grow where the barley was planted last year. The trees in the copse are in sticky bud and the hedgerows are white with frothy hawthorn. Bees shimmer amid the pink clover. The breeze is laced with dynamite, petrol and sweat. Stumps are blasted, ground levelled. Swarms of men tend machines, which rip and smash through the hedges and undergrowth. The earth is spewed and flattened under the treads of bull-dozers. Day and night, night and day, in muddy shifts, an aerodrome is built. From reveille to taps the men sing, as they work, as they mooch and jostle in the chow line.

Jesu, Lord, Ain't dat a thing, Come back Baby.

Look now, as squadrons of bombers roar in, with a fresh crop of men. Government issue, grown in America, harvested over here. Green faces, loose bowels; wisecracking, resolute. Lucky medallions buttoned into flying jackets; letters and keepsakes left under the pillow. It never gets any easier, as crew after crew take to the sky. Count them out, count them home. Sweat it out, in the hangars with the mechanics. Squint up at the sky. Wait, as the hands of the clock eke out the day. Wait, as the tousle eared mascot whines and shakes, keeping vigil for his crew.

Feel the goosebumps prickle the shoulders of the naked girl under the army blanket, hear her sigh as she sloughs off the shop girl and reinvents herself as his fantasy, just for an hour. *Never want this war to end*. Feel the bloody resignation of the ground crew, sluicing the splattered, shattered fuselage. The tarmac runs red. Tonight there are spaces in the pub where men stood yesterday and tomorrow there will be new faces at breakfast.

But on a day like today, when the air is untroubled by eddies from the past, the shrill pipe of a curlew on the wing is the only accompaniment to the clinking links of the fence.

Keep out! Property of the Ministry of Defence, remnants of wartime enclosure. Nothing to see here, a barren stretch of concrete branded onto the landscape. A colony of weeds fighting through the cracks in the runway and a snarl of gorse insinuating its way into the fence. An empty space.

The Student New Angle Prize Runner Up North Sea, Over Night by Jayd Green

My story is inspired by the story of the man who worked the night shift at Lowestoft Lighthouse near Ness Point during the flood in 1953. I attended an event at The Hold in Ipswich where there were several talks about the flood not just its historical importance, but also looking at the future flood risks and sea defences. Two images stayed with me after the various presentations - the nightwatchman being less concerned about being rescued from his stranded position than someone being able to take over when his shift ended, and that after the flood, seagulls were seen diving and eating the worms that had drowned in the soil of the gardens and nearby fields. There were no recorded casualties in Lowestoft, but I wanted to include the sense of loss and confusion that accompanies natural disaster.

North Sea, Over Night by Jayd Green

The man who will watch through the night at Ness Point clocks in for his shift.

Nothing is wrong yet - the water stretches out, closes the horizon. The sea ripples in a way that looks like settling.

The police burst into the pub at Gas Works Road. The door billows with rain, the streetlight flickers above them. Though many voices are speaking, not a word or a language can be identified in the room. Still, there is the miracle of understanding.

The night watchman has been fretting, and is busy with it. The sea stretches closer and beyond him, and yet it is not languid. He begins to understand what this creeping in really means - part of it is stranding him. The other part is being in this lighthouse, following the beam and hoping to find a fraction of the landscape that existed there a few hours ago.

He cannot believe anything will still be there when the sea resigns, rescinds, rewinds. He does not ask for rescue - only whether the day watch will still come when his shift ends.

Then there is the next day. He smokes, and drinks whisky from a bottle he found floating alongside him as he steered the dingy. He is in his mother's house which is empty, except for the claustrophobia of items where they do not belong. Strange things have washed in through the windows: a clock, a barrel of herring wedged in the fireplace, a cat.

Seagulls glide softly from roof to garden. They scavenge and fight over drowned worms which have risen to the surface of water, which is not pond, not river, not ocean. Only *flood*, a word of quiet chaos.

The Student New Angle Prize Highly Commended
Fire in the Sky by Muriel Moore-Smith

One summer holiday many years ago I stayed with my family for a few nights at Theberton on the Suffolk coast. Whilst out walking, we came across St Peter's church, and were fascinated by an account of the crashing of a Zeppelin on display in its porch. It relayed the fact that in June 1917 a German Zeppelin had been shot by artillery near Orford, quickly becoming an inferno and eventually falling to land in a field near the village. The story was enhanced by the display of a fire-damaged fragment of the frame of the airship and a memorial to the seventeen German airmen who died in the crash. The story has stayed with me over the years, and I have often thought about the audacity of sending unwieldy Zeppelins from northern Germany all those miles to the English coast. What an uncanny spectacle it must have been to see a huge, burning craft in the June sky over the bleached Suffolk fields. And what bravery it must have taken for the German airmen to participate in a long, perilous trip into the unknown. In doing further research for this story, I was moved to read that at a memorial service marking the one-hundred-year anniversary of the crash, a candle was lit for each of the crew and for the men of Theberton who lost their lives in the First World War.

Fire in the Sky by Muriel Moore-Smith

It is the creaking and whooshing above him which first alerts him to it. Later, he had wondered whether he was able to discern the cries of men amidst the noise, but no, in truth he could only recall the roar of flames and the whistling of air as the ship sliced its way through the sky.

The fire overhead illuminates the entire garden, passing so low that he thinks it will set Mother's washing alight. Great black smuts rain down on white sheets. He feels intense heat on the top of his head and raises his eyes, squinting against the raging fireball which has just now jettisoned part of itself in the field.

Zeppelin, breathes the boy. *Here, over my garden, a German Zeppelin*. He ponders the incongruity of it for a moment, calculates how many miles it must have travelled to get here, then remembers the dry, yellow fields, the hay-bales lazing in the Suffolk sun. The whole lot'll go up like a tinder box.

He starts to run, vaults the garden fence, stumbles momentarily on the rock-hard ground. His legs and arms are well-oiled pistons as he sprints along the coastal path. Ahead of him, the vast hull of the Zeppelin stutters, an orange lozenge, towards the earth.

A crash, then a ricochet of sound, like the dry air has been concertinaed. The ground vibrates beneath his feet.

He is first on the scene, although only for a matter of

moments; there are shouts behind him as a swarm of men on bicycles arrive carrying a hosepipe between them. *Boy! Quick! Where's the nearest well?* It is a short journey home to the well, the boy running, the men following along behind. Some douse the livid flames with water, others dodge the heat and smoke looking for survivors. *Look!* The boy shouts, seeing a body roll from under the orange glow of the girders, his fur coat dancing with flames. He watches as the man is bundled into the back of an ambulance, the fur coat now a blackened hide. Others are less fortunate: charred beings, curled in on themselves, no longer human. He looks at his boots as they are carried past. *Try not to worry*, says a man behind him, placing a warm, heavy hand on his shoulder. *They'll all be given a Christian burial.* He nods and thinks of his father, fighting somewhere in France. There'd been no letter for weeks.

In the grainy light of dusk, the Zeppelin now lies like the sun-bleached skeleton of a great whale, the people dotted around it miniscule, ridiculous against its magnitude. Tired now but reluctant to leave the spectacle, the boy creeps forward and picks up a fragment of iron girder. It lies hot in his hand. Carefully, he wraps it in a handkerchief and puts it in his pocket. Walking home, he feels its warmth pulse in syncopation with his own heartbeat, like something made alive by fire.

When his father returns home, he too will have a story to tell.

The Student New Angle Prize
Shortlisted writers

Guardian by Nic Whittam

My story was inspired by two strands of my Granny-in-law's life. To distinguish her from other grannies we called her Granny Pat-a-cake. My children shortened that to Patacake, and thus she is and will always be Patacake. As a child, Patacake was briefly evacuated from London to Orford.

After narrowly escaping death in a bombing raid, she was recalled to London where she lived for the remainder of the war. However, the brief time spent in Suffolk marked her heart. She had met her future husband there and eventually found her way back to him. They lived all their married lives in Aldeburgh, including through the 1953 floods, with a small daughter (my mother-in-law). Spiritualist beliefs were strong in Patacake's maternal line and despite never having met Great-Granny-in-law (though she lived until she was 112) I was aware of her presence casting something of a shadow over the lives of her daughter and granddaughter. This is a story based on true events, but not necessarily in the right order.

Guardian by Nic Whittam

I don't remember the before times. I know I was there though, a small child running around getting under everyone's feet. Then there is the aftermath, that I do remember. The event itself that's crystal clear.

Mother said it was cold, very cold, blizzard like. She was always prone to exaggeration, but I don't doubt that it was cold – it was January in Aldeburgh after all. The winds from the east bite and when they join with those from the north, they brutally assault you. Marry that with a tide of which we'd never known the like, and we have a storm made for ending souls.

We knew it was coming. Mother said the days before passed in a blur of preparations. 'The Surge' was coming, we didn't know just how much of it was coming. Fishermen and the people who live with them and love them, know to be wary of the sea, especially when it tries to take the land. But you weren't a fisherman, you were a painter. And I didn't even like fish. I still don't like to look at them, they are too knowing with their unblinking gaze.

I must have gone to bed as usual, maintaining the rites and rituals, talking to the guardians, securing their favours. Granny had instilled a fear, respect she called it, of the spirits and I always spoke to them before bed to ask them for their protection. I still do.

The water came. At first it snuck silently under the door,

early sentinels searching out weaknesses, finding gaps in our preparations. Then it pounced and we were inundated. All the work that everyone had done, undone in a blink.

Mother told me that Granny refused to leave without her coat. It was quickly lost downstairs in the swirling, stinking, surging blackness that had been our cosy living room. There was an argument in the loft about sitting on the roof, climbing above the encroaching water, and attracting rescue. It was, Granny said, not decorous for a lady to be outside in her dressing-gown. Granny said she might as well be naked. Mother told her that if she didn't leave now, she needn't worry about her reputation. I have an inkling that stronger words of encouragement were used. Mother told me that she'd said the spirits would scoff at Granny and ridicule her for being so hoity and giving up everything she had for a coat. That thrashed a nerve, I can tell you. I can still feel it jangling, even now.

Rescue came, not to all, but to us.

You waved as the waves engulfed you. I didn't think you meant to leave, but looking back, I think that was why you were here. My house painter, my home maker. I didn't know that you were the guardian I prayed to whilst I knelt beside you. You held me calm in a sea of panic. You did what you were here to do, and then you left.

Kensington Gardens by Sophie Wilks

When I began writing Kensington Gardens, I intended to write a story that highlights one of the forgotten gems of Lowestoft. I was inspired to write the feeling that magical beings can exist in the most mundane places. Kensington Gardens is a place that, like a lot of Lowestoft, has lost its magic over the years and I hoped to regain some of that in my writing. With every piece I write, my goal is always to bring enchantment back to my hometown.

Kensington Gardens by Sophie Wilks

Walking along the pier, Kensington Gardens rose up beside me. It's a part of Lowestoft that doesn't look like it should be there. A canopy of trees sheltered a bridge and an algae-covered pond. I can't remember when the water was last clear, running as fake a blue as the boating pond in the entranceway, shining like melted slushie in the sun.

From the gated entrance, you could look out at Lowestoft seafront, the clean lines of the grey concrete wall, the yellow sand atop it and the sea stacked further to each other like Neapolitan ice cream. Grey, yellow, blue.

The sky was completely clear, cleansed of clouds and chemtrails, so the water below ran in its natural colour. A spectrum of green and brown, crested by small waves that rose and crashed against itself in a rolling motion that collided in my ears.

There was summer in the air, carrying the laughs of children and the ring of the ice cream van. With it came the feeling of having so much time to do anything, drink, relax, and sit on the floor and not wonder where you have to be. I sat with my legs crossed so that the gravel dug into the side of my knees. The sun even melted away the pain that radiated in the small of my back, nature's *Deep Heat*.

I felt like a child there. I sat on the floor and felt the tiny stones bite into the back of my legs and dirt pressed into my dress, but I wasn't worried about the stains. That was the spirit of summer. I could feel it falling through the stress, liquid sunlight filtered through an awning of emerald leaves, each one veined with it. I felt it lick my skin, the paleness of winter replaced by a tan only I could see.

This seemed just the place for fairies. They hid within the shrubbery in the maze of twigs and rubbish, invisible to the naked eye. My eyes flicked across the bushes, watching for a flit of wings. With the expertise of a child, I built a dress around my finger, wrapping a thick waxy leaf to fit a fairy-sized waist and cutting a hole with my nail through the back to make it hold together, threading the stalk into a knot. The skirt I assembled was much the same. Attaching everything with a loop and the stem made the leaf into a belt around the middle. I placed them into the hollow of the undergrowth, hoping they'd be taken away by a set of little hands.

Littleport 1815 by Mike Laurence

The story of the drainage and enclosure of the Fens has always struck me as an historical tragedy. The haunting quality of the Fenland landscape is bound up with its past. The superficial observer sees flat fields and ditches as far as the horizon, with the odd house, pylon or dilapidated farm building creating scale. Behind this bleak landscape lies a very different world. Rich dark soil tempted those wishing to control the land to dispossess its inhabitants, to tame the winding rivers, and push back the tides.

While living and working in the area I became fascinated by its history, and learnt to read the landscape, with the help of maps and historical accounts, identifying insignificant banks and ditches as evidence of the huge changes which unfolded over centuries, as the ancient way of life became marginalised and demonised, the marshes drained and its people derided as web-footed 'yellow bellies.' The Littleport riots were amongst the last acts of resistance against the forced destruction of an ancient way of life, occurring at the same time as the native peoples of North America and Australia were being exterminated.

Littleport, 1815 by Mike Laurence

Samuel was one of the few who spoke out. The threat of French invasion seemed to take the fight out of so many in the village. The landlords, increasingly nameless men from far away had no sympathy for the Fenland ways, the seasonal changes that allowed Samuel and his neighbours to live a good life. The commons were essential for grazing, fishing, peat digging, their land.

All now under threat. Drainage works and forced enclosure was depriving the village of its simple livelihoods. Occasional temporary work for the landlord would not sustain his growing family.

They'd tried to resist, challenged their right to take the land, pleaded to the local lords, prayed at church.

Some had been more direct, tearing down fences, fighting the workers brought in to do the enclosing, traveling to the local town to protest, banging pots, shouting, even throwing stones. Some men had already been arrested; rumour was sent to Australia in irons.

Their scrappy little cottage sat in the rain, mossy thatch, and a muddy path.

They had no money, and the children were thin and pale. Samuel and Mary sat in front of the peat fire that never went out. The smoky room was dark except for a faint red glow.

'What about working the harvest?'

'That's months away, we need food now, and the rent.'

Samuel spoke in a low voice. Years of seeing this coming had affected him more than he realized. Some had curled up and refused to see the truth and had been driven from their homes. The hedgerow dwellers were now a common site. Hungry children hanging out by the church, begging for your conscience. Some villages had a house for the poor but not theirs. The vicar was in with the local Gentry, looked down on their sort. He'd officiate out of duty, they had married in his church, had the children baptized there, but that meant little when you came to his door asking for help. It was God's will that you were poor.

Sam spat in the fire. He had to say it.

'I'll have to go. Maybe London.'

'We'll never see you again, that place, you'll be a lost soul.'

'Well, what about Lynn? There's the docks. I'm strong still, can turn a day's work.'

Mary sighed, looked up at him.

'I don't want to lose you. Promise you'll get word back, come back when you can.'

Sam murmured 'of course,' knowing how hard it was to promise. A week later he was on the road. They had had a tearful last meal, he hugged all the children, the smallest clung to his leg.

He set off at dawn, after a sleepless night. Mary walked a little way on the road with him. The new dyke flowed slowly beside them, draining their world. They held each other. A wave at the corner, and he looked ahead.

Winterton Pups by Jeni Neill

On one of the days following Christmas, when bellies feel a bit fuller and time, if fortunate, is our own, my family went to Winterton-on-Sea to blow the year's cobwebs away. Our large group, having had the treat of all being home for Christmas, included toddler grandchildren and two of our dogs. It was such a memorable walk because we were all there and because, in the magic of that late afternoon air, treasured memories were created.

Dusk was at our heels and other walkers were beginning to thin, but a warden, looking after the numerous seal pups along the sand, kept his watch. He answered all our questions so patiently and we felt so grateful that he, voluntarily, acted to protect these vulnerable creatures from over-curious human and canine dangers. Inspired by the scene and the knowledge he shared, I wrote 'Winterton Pups' on our return.

Winterton Pups by Jeni Neill

On this wide horizon of sea and sand
framed by sky and foreground dune,
birthed pups, tones of grey, black, white
blend with their nature's hue.

Dotted heaps along miles of fringe,
scattered pairs or solo mounds:
Three weeks of milk support is all they'll know
before being left completely alone.

Find me, find me -
an anxious plea on the wind,
to the giant, sleek pelt that slithers to land,
delivered on thrashing waves and spray of North Sea.

As she inhales the map of her shore,
diluted by human and canine scents,
I momentarily doubt her innate skill
to define her particular pup once more.

Shore line shifting and moving at pace,
with eroding coastline crumbling down.
Scenery changing but here, in this place,
these creatures remind us of the patterns to trust.

Moon takes over from the white hidden sun,
their abandonment sharp in the shadows of dusk.
Lifeless pups wasting for gulls' checking pecks,
whilst survivors wait for the change in their coats.

Life only detected by a flap of a tail,
or lift of a head bearing huge watery eyes -
the poster pinniped look, making us feel
they're a cuddly friend who feels as we do.

In zeros that shudder our weaker thin skins,
we pull hoods over heads and scarf further up
whilst they lie exposed in the barest of scenes,
as if being prepared, like a tested Marine.

Changing milk sucking comfort for the life they must own
in dark depths of currents,
group rivalry and seasonal change await in their tides –
as does the freedom and grace of the glide.

Writers' Biographies

Daisy Woollerton

Daisy Woollerton is a writer living in north Suffolk. She enjoys dark fantasy, sci-fi and folk lore and is currently writing a YA novel.

Daisy is studying MA Creative and Critical Writing at the University of Suffolk. When she's not writing or studying, she is gaming, enjoying the east Suffolk beaches and being pestered by her three lovely but needy cats.

Jayd Green

Jayd Green is a writer living in Norwich. She is currently a PhD candidate with the University of Suffolk, and Editorial Advisor for experimental poetry publisher, *Osmosis Press*. Her poems have appeared in *Anthropocene*, *Foliate Oak* literary magazine and *Royal Rose*, and Footprints: An Anthology of New Ecopoetry by *Broken Sleep Books*. Her writing and research are concerned with contemporary nature writing practices, ecocriticism, and the ecogothic. Her twitter handle is @jaydgreen

Daniel Snowling

Daniel Snowling is a lecturer in creative media at East Coast College. He received his Bachelor of Arts in Arts

Practice from the University of Suffolk and is currently completing his MA in Creative and Critical Writing there too. He has a love of film and an interest in telling stories that deal with the mystical, mythological, and mysterious; stories that explore both fantasy and reality. When he's not working or studying, he can be found writing screenplays in his office with a cup of tea, surrounded by biscuits, usually hobnobs.

Molly-Kate Britton

Molly-Kate Britton has completed her BA and MA at the University of Suffolk, and is now a Creative Writing PhD student there, working on a novel about Alma Mahler. Her interests lie in historical fiction, as well as neo-gothic fiction. She loves to write and travel, as well as bake and embroider.

Kizzy Barrow

Kizzy is a writer, gardener and visual artist living in Suffolk. They grew up within the New Traveller community and their work is informed by a non-traditional exploration of the natural world and is concerned with land justice and environmental futurity. Their work inhabits mediums such as traditional textile crafts, prose, poetry, and song. Their work includes Bénévoles, a photo essay documenting displaced communities in Northern France, which was exhibited in 2019 with an accompanying chapbook. Kizzy is currently working on a collection of contemporary folk stories that seeks to unite historical and present-day experiences of landscape and resistance.

Charlotte Yule

Charlotte is a writer and postgraduate student living in rural Suffolk. She has worked in publishing and leads youth outreach projects which promote equitable writing experiences for young people in isolated coastal regions. She has had work published in 'Modern Nature,' a Derek Jarman inspired anthology and is co-editing an anthology of Suffolk queer voices. After graduating from her MA in August, Charlotte will pursue a PhD at Birkbeck University of London.

Ellen Freeman

Ellen Freeman is an author and poet from Suffolk. She is a Writer in Residence at the Van Gogh Museum Amsterdam, and is currently working on a collection of essays and poetry inspired by the artist's life. Ellen was shortlisted for the Canterbury Festival Fiction Prize in 2022 and longlisted for the New Angle Fiction Prize in 2023. Ellen is currently studying MA Creative and Critical Writing at the University of Suffolk. She graduated from the Open University's BA English Literature and Creative Writing programme in 2021. Ellen is the author of two middle grade fantasy novels and is currently working on a Greek Mythology retelling. In her spare time, Ellen runs book-related social media pages, and buys more books than she could ever possibly read.

Charlie Brodie

Charlie Brodie is a writer based in Norfolk but has predominately studied in Suffolk. They have previously worked as a Co-Editor for the LGBT segment of Student Life and spend most of their time writing stories that are focused on queer youth and life. Charlie is currently studying on the MA Creative and Critical Writing at the University of Suffolk and is writing a novel that is a queer adaptation of Shakespeare's Romeo and Juliet. They are partnering with The Hold in Ipswich to curate and showcase an art exhibition that highlights Suffolk Queer Voices. Charlie is also co-editing a queer anthology of UOS students and alumni.

Mike Laurence

Mike Laurence is a retired GP living in South Norfolk. He is currently an MA student of Creative and Critical Writing at the University of Suffolk. His GP career was merely a 50-year interlude between English A Level and his current studies, and he is enjoying lighting up areas of his brain that lay dormant for all that time.

Claire Holland

Claire Holland is a writer living in Suffolk. She has had short stories published in *Suffolk Arboretum* and the children's anthology *Rebels with a Very Good Cause*. In 2023 she had her short story, *Home, Suffolk* longlisted for the Student New Angle Prize. Claire is in her final year of the MA in Creative and Critical Writing at the University of Suffolk and is currently writing a crime novel set in East Anglia. In her spare time, she enjoys reading crime fiction and creating unique pieces of jewellery from recycled silver. Claire resides in Suffolk with her husband and two daughters.

Muriel Moore-Smith

Muriel Moore-Smith is a writer and singer who lives in Suffolk with her husband and three daughters. She studied literature at the University of Leeds, completed an MA in Literature (Woman Writing) at the University of Essex before being lured to the sunny climes of California where she gained an MFA in vocal performance from the University of California, Irvine. She is currently studying for a PhD in Creative Writing at the University of Suffolk, where she a writing a piece of historical fiction, *H's code*, based on the life of her great grandfather. A lover of stories in all their guises, Muriel is particularly interested in the various opportunities writing presents to make sense of past lives and histories and the writer's obligations in this process.

Emillie Simmons

Emillie Simmons is an MA Critical and Creative Writing student at UoS who enjoys reading and writing crime fiction. She is writing a crime novel as part of her studies. She is also hoping to continue her studies with a second MA in Writing Crime Fiction at The University of East Anglia. She enjoys writing horror, and adaptations - one being an adaptation of the Prom scene in Stephen King's *Carrie*. This is a different genre and style of writing for Emillie, but she has thoroughly enjoyed taking part in this anthology.

Sarah Waterson

Sarah Waterson is a writer who has enjoyed writing since childhood. In primary school, her favourite lesson was creative writing. Over the years she has written short stories, poems and has two novels planned out. Sarah has also co-run and hosted small writing groups, too. Her dad always encouraged her to write, and he 'commissioned' her to write a short story in return for a box of red wine of her choice! Sarah plans to get some of her work published after she completes her MA in Creative and Critical Writing at the University of Suffolk.

Jeni Neill

East Anglia is intrinsic to Jeni Neill, having spent her childhood in the Fens, formative years in Suffolk and then, later, settling with her own family in Norfolk. Four years ago, she felt driven to begin to write and form the ideas that had been brewing for many years, increasingly pressing for air. In 2020, she self-published *The Devil's Dye*, a locally set historical fiction novel. The following year, she produced a collection of short stories, *Fen Roads*, and enjoys giving talks about the creation of these books to local societies and libraries. She is currently studying the MA in Creative and Critical Writing at the University of Suffolk, where course content and tutor guidance has helped identify her passion for both socio-political study and the fictional, magical realism. Her poem *Winterton Pups* was short-listed for the Student New Angle Prize 2023. Working from home, she cherishes time spent with her husband, four children and two grandchildren, as well as their modest menagerie of animals.

Luke Mayo

Luke Mayo is a long-time member of the University of Suffolk English Department, having graduated with a BA (Hons) in English in 2016. He is a part of the 2022-2023 cohort of the MA in Creative and Critical Writing. Luke has always been interested in literary pursuits. He has blogged extensively for the *Global Panorama* (as a writer and editor for the Arts Section), written a highly commended poem for the South Essex College Creative Writing Challenge and had two poetry collections published with Book Leaf Publishing, for which he received an Emily Dickinson Award in 2022. Luke has also completed two series of his podcast, *Mayo's Musings*.

Amber Spalding

Amber Spalding enjoys all forms of writing, but gravitates towards experimental nature writing, familial narratives, and poetry. She is in her final year of studying for the MA in Creative and Critical Writing at the University of Suffolk and is currently working on her first novel. Outside of her studies, Amber is a committee member for the Suffolk Book League and a poetry editor for the online literary magazine, *Incognito Press*. Her writing is featured in the MA's previous anthologies: *Suffolk Folk: An Anthology of East Anglian Tales for the 21st Century*, and *Suffolk Arboretum: An Anthology of East Anglian Stories Inspired by Remarkable Trees*.

Gabrielle Stones

Gabrielle Stones is a librarian by day, and a writer by night, living in Suffolk. When she isn't encouraging the younger generation to fall in love with books and keeping the library fully stocked, she is writing poetry, and has recently taken a liking to writing prose over the course of her MA in Creative and Critical Writing, at the University of Suffolk. After being commended for her poem, '12:03' in the Woodbridge Young Poets competition, she has been fascinated by anything poetic, and is always eager to use her creativity to write new poems. In her spare time, she likes to read as much as she can, to get through her large to be read list!

Amber Atkinson

Amber Atkinson currently writes creatively for her blog, *The Seven Year Itch* and enjoys writing ghost stories, with one featured on the SNAP Short List in 2020. Amber is currently working towards her MA in Creative and Critical Writing at the University of Suffolk, with further plans to undertake a PhD.

Laura Cockhill

Laura Cockhill is a writer living on the borders of Suffolk. She studied Creative Writing as an Undergraduate at Liverpool John Moores University and was the 2012 winner of The Edmund Cusick Avalon Prize. Laura is currently studying on the MA Creative and Critical Writing at the University of Suffolk and enjoys writing both prose and poetry. She hopes to one day become a successful literary agent. She is a former vintage clothing dealer and lives happily beside the sea with her son and their two French Bulldogs, Luna, and Balthazar.

Anya Page

Anya Page is a writer, Francophile, cookery enthusiast, and former international asset finance lawyer. She is currently studying toward an MA in History at the University of Suffolk. Anya's research interests include twentieth century social history, genealogy, and newspapers. She is a keen reader of historical fiction and partial to a good crime novel.

Nic Whittam

Absorbed in her own experience of the world, too excited and enthusiastic to be swayed by anyone's reticence, not always noticing the perils until they're past – and then doing her best not to dwell on them – Nic is all heart and thoughtfulness. Strangers are surprised to hear she's studying for an MSc in Data Science and AI, but she revels in defying expectations and pushing herself out of her comfort zone. Her motto is 'it's all about the edges,' because the edges are where we are at our most vulnerable, and where we learn most about ourselves.

Creative Writing at the University of Suffolk

The MA Creative and Critical Writing at the University of Suffolk, offers you the opportunity to join a vibrant writing community and focus on your passion for creative writing whilst engaging with the most up-to-date debates in critical theory.

On the course, you will nurture and develop skills as a creative writer, reader and researcher, broadening your knowledge of the production and reception of literature under the supervision of qualified academics and award-winning authors. You will experience an integrated approach to creative writing and contemporary developments in critical and cultural theories while exploring a range of established and evolving literary genres, such as historical fiction, memoir, and children's literature. To find out more please go to:

https://www.uos.ac.uk/courses/pg/
ma-creative-and-critical-writing

OTHER ANTHOLOGIES AVAILABLE FROM THE TALKING SHOP PRESS

SUFFOLK FOLK
East Anglian Folk Tales for the 21st Century.

In this collection of old tales re-visioned for contemporary readers, East Anglia's green children, mermaids, malekins and monsters come together with the secret lives of fairies and the power of lost-loves, making bold new stories that leap, hagstone in hand, into modern life.

SUFFOLK ARBORETUM
Original Stories Inspired by Remarkable Trees.

It is possible to find every tree or area of woodland featured in these stories. We recommend you take a tour of Suffolk with the anthology in hand and find each tree, from Haverhill to Lowestoft. Sit in the dappled shade of green canopies and read the original writing that our county's woodlands inspired.

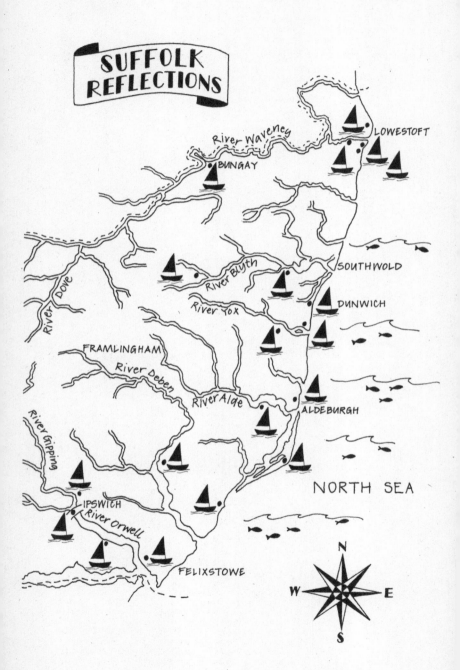